The Cannibal's Guide to Ethical Living

The Cannibal's Guide to Ethical Living

by

MYKLE HANSEN

Illustrated by Nate Beaty

Eraserhead Press
Portland, OR

ERASERHEAD PRESS
205 NE BRYANT
PORTLAND, OR 97211

WWW.ERASERHEADPRESS.COM

ISBN: 1-936383-28-4

Cover art & caligraphy by Keegan Onefoot
Interior illustrations by Nate Beaty

Printed in the USA.

Gracious thanks are due
to David Thierry Knox
for the French,
to Dan Burt for the title,
and to Jon, Megan, Seth and Missy
for the parking.

This book is dedicated
to QUARTÉ,
JERROTÉ,
and NAPOLEON.

Menu

Aspic Sweetbreads of Heiress Dissolu—7

Domaine Tempier Rosé, Bandol, 2009—21

Plat de Charcuterie—37

Mock Oxtail Soup—49

Pearls Before Swine (Jewelled Roast of Millionairess)—61

Beet Pickled Eyes—73

Knuckles Poutine à la Pommes Frites—89

Plat au Fromage—105

Quebec Ragoût de Pattes et Avant-Bras—131

Louis Roederer Cristal Brut, 1916—149

Dessert Juste—161

I've got to stop eating millionaires.

Wake up, Louis, open your eyes. You're safe now. The bad man is gone, the gunfire and the screaming have stopped, the natives have surrendered the pier and withdrawn to the shore. A big storm is coming, a mighty force of nature; it's clamped a truce on these current events. Nobody dares go topside—the millionaires' yachts are fleeing the harbor, anchoring themselves offshore, battening down to wait it out. The islanders are backing slowly, angrily up the beach, back to the shelter of their little lump, that poor excuse for high ground they call Mont Cristobo. Crushing waves and hellacious wind are coming to slap down everything we've built here. L'Arche, our happy floating bistro, is closed for lunch.

But you're safe here for now. No need for trembling, no need for whimpering and cringing. Just open them, Louis. Show me your beautiful eyes. This is not the sight you might have hoped for, but it's certainly worth a peek.

Welcome to our abattoir. Sorry it's such a shambles; pardon the blood everywhere, and never mind the rats. Of course if you'd warned me you were coming I would have swept up a bit, scrubbed things down, polished the crucifix, perhaps hung some art. Believe me, it's never this messy; we've just been so *busy*. It was only yesterday that Marko brought in our last bit of business, and thereby lit the burners under us all.

Louis ... are you weeping?

Well, yes, it is a sad thing, Louis. You really have no idea what I'm giving up. Millionaires are exquisitely delicious! Their flesh has a sweet, rich, yielding texture to which nothing compares. Their oiled and pampered skin, stratified with wealthy fat, crisps up under moderate heat like the most delicate pastry dough. In the kitchen, they are magic.

I see it in your eyes, you're dubious. But before you leave this place I will prepare for you my Millionaire in Limousine: steaming roasted loin of venture capitalist slow-braised in Madeira, served on a bed of squid-ink cabbage poached with chestnuts and Lardons Millionaires. You've never had anything like it. I also insist you try my Aspic Sweetbreads of Heiress Dissolu, molded in a swine's head terrine and tiaraed with clove and apple. So light and delicate, you'd think it's made of perfumed dreams.

You don't believe me now, Louis—you've heard the bragging of the great chefs, I know, and yes we are proud and puffed-up sons of bitches—but you will. This is no mere restaurant—it's a cathedral of food! Pilgrims to l'Arche have by our rare and exquisite flavors been transported, transmigrated, have communed with the great mystery, have wept with joy, have been saved.

Louis ... you're not smiling. Aren't you glad to see me?

Please don't think I'm angry with you, Louis. I'm thrilled that you've come, that you sniffed me out. But your timing, I regret, is off by just one day! Tomorrow I am forced to retire. I hate to, but I have to. Alas, I'll never have the pleasure of hosting you on the dining deck with proper linens and proper service. Our waitstaff has abandoned ship, along with the dishwasher. Once our kitchen comrades, they now hurl stones at us from the shore.

And you, Louis, have come halfway across the world to see me! I want to show you everything I can in this brief time remaining before the curtain falls. I owe it to you, old friend.

It's a world-changing discovery: in millionaires I truly believe I have discovered nature's perfect food. More than just delicious, when paired with a good wine they are eminently digestible and fortifying. I'm the proof! For the last three booming months, as a rising tide of popularity tossed and heaved our little ship l'Arche, as Salome and Marko and I stretched ourselves over fifteen and twenty hour shifts of hard kitchen labor, night after night, to please a torrent of hypercritical guests, slicing and sauteing and reducing, par-boiling and butchering and boning—so much boning, Louis! Forever stripping out bone after incriminating, stubborn, well-bred bone—oh Louis, it's been crazy. At my age I couldn't have done it without the help of millionaires.

I'll have you know that for over a year I have subsisted on a diet of pure millionaires, harvested fresh from clean and spacious yachts, plucked from the ripe apex of the food chain. Aside from an occasional breakfast of cold giraffe and fruit salad, that's all I've had. Millionaire meat is rich and well-marbled, but not once have I felt stomach aches, constipation, gas, lethargy or any of those Atkins diet symptoms.

Nor, might I add, have I felt those miserable pangs of guilt and complicity that garnish the sickening meat produced in the industrial flesh factories. The ongoing wholesale torture of captive chickens, pigs and calves: everything I know of it revolts me, Louis. I will not serve such food. But I have never needed to lie to myself about the mistreatment of these millionaires. They were not raised in stacked boxes, unable to stand, injected with growth hormones and forced to shit upon one another. Millionaires are the definition of free-ranging; they're as ethically clean as they are flavorful and nutritious.

In a word, they are wholesome. They satisfy and fortify. In the last year of eating millionaires I haven't wept one tear or farted one note. Look at me, Louis! Look at these hands! I'm strong! Full of life! Energy and vigor, I've never had more! They're a goddamn fountain of youth, these delicious, vitamin-rich, polyunsaturated locally-sourced free-range millionaires!

And now I've got to give them up. It is a goddamn shame.

Perhaps I was a fool to think it could last. But why couldn't it? Overfishing isn't a problem; I never once imagined we'd run low of the bastards. Doesn't it seem there are more of them yachting around every day? You've seen them, Louis. You've been to their hideaways, their special places: all their country lodges on private

13

property ringed with color-coded militia, all their mid-eastern luxury hotels staffed with Filipino slaves, all their orbiting bistros and gourmet submarines. In my thirty years in the kitchen I've never known such a positive plague of millionaires! Cut down one, two more are freshly minted in place.

In fact, in this woeful era of ours where everything good and clean seems to be withering, dying off, drying out and blowing away—the oceans, the farms, the forests, life of all kinds, human life especially—there is only one healthy, thriving megafauna left on earth to feed the future: millionaires.

It's hard to imagine that one or two of them would be missed.

Oh Louis! Your Gallic eyes are so expressive. You are thinking: of course they'd be missed! They have families, personal assistants, chauffeurs, household managers, friendly neighboring millionaires, et cetera. The police, even. You are thinking: they can't just vanish and be forgotten, ripped from the gilded tapestry of their millionaire lives without questions asked, curiosities piqued. Even here, in this forgotten southern part of the world with such a rich and poignant history of disappearances political, narcotic, extra-terrestrial and otherwise. You are thinking: tragedies like that don't happen any more.

Oh, Louis. You've even met Marko, and still you believe such things.

On the topic of Marko, that fascinating and complex man, my semi-silent partner and captain of this vessel—oh, I could say so much about Marko, so many stories and I dare say we'll have time for a few, but first and foremost: I am sorry. Sorry about Marko, sorry about all that ugly business upstairs. Sorry our reunion is stained by such brutality. I witnessed it: it was rude, it was cruel, it was a goddamn collapse of my well-honed hospitality. How's the bleeding? Slowed down some, I hope? But look at you: your suit's rumpled, your bow tie's askew, your nerves are frayed and tangled. Shivering like that, so wide-eyed and silent, with your round hairless head and your scimitar nose, you resemble a trussed-up dove—a desecrated herald of peace!

I'm so sorry, Louis. There will be consequences, I promise you. I fear I'll be apologizing all night; none of this is the welcome you deserve ... but rejoice! You are my guest now, again as so many times before. And the comfort of my guests is my first concern.

Sadly, regarding certain of your discomforts, my hands are just as tied as yours—albeit by caution and strategy instead of cheesecloth and twine. Again, I'm sorry, but I will do what I can.

15

For a start, may I rid you of that uncomfortable, humiliating gag that Marko tied around your head? It doesn't suit a man of your stature. I can have it off you in a jiffy. All I need in return, Louis, is your promise.

Let me explain the situation we find ourselves in. Marko, that massive, empty-eyed bear of a man you encountered so recently in the kitchen, is lurking up there still. He sulks, he fires occasional bullets at the shore, he fondles the knives. He's just been lightly shot, nothing serious but it's certainly affected his mood. In all the time I've known him, I've never seen him so Markoish as today. He's worried, and rightly so. He's tripped a trap that's snared us all, and his animal cunning is not finding him an exit. He's a dangerous man at the best of times, our Marko, but right now he's boiling oil; one more piece of bad news could ignite him like a grease fire. And he's just recently given me the task of dissolving you in butter—

Louis ... please, relax. Banging around on the floor, making noise, all of this trying-to-escape business, that is exactly the *wrong* thing to do, don't you get it? Get a grip, Louis ... let's get you back on the stool.

Louis, I know what you're thinking. Please, stop trembling and look at me. Look in my eyes, and put those frightening, foolish thoughts out of your head.

You have my word as a gentleman: I promise not to eat you.

I'm sure you've wondered, from that moment you felt Marko's thick hand clutch your spine when he caught you snapping pictures of the soup bones, whether you'd be next for the pot. And then arriving here in this dramatic little room: knives on the table, hooks on the ceiling, bones on the floor, blood all around, Our Holy Headwaiter crucified and glaring on the wall ... the goddamn rats everywhere ... of course you assumed the worst, of course you fainted. You know what I'm like.

But please, put yourself at ease and just let me host you. I promise you gentleness, good cheer and all the safety I can muster.

The truth is, Louis: we're both in a bit of a pickle—myself for complicated reasons I'll explain in due course, and you by mere association. (Your timing, I'll say just once more, is *awful*.) But I have a plan for our mutual salvation, Louis, that doesn't involve eating you or anyone else with a net worth of less than one million dollars. It requires, mostly, that we wait.

But we've got to wait discreetly. You've got to adopt the mind-set of the stowaway. We're deep underwater here, two decks below the kitchen, but sounds can travel in these old ships.

If we keep to this quiet level of conversation we're having now, just a stage whisper, then I believe we'll be safe. But if Marko were to learn you're still breathing, and enjoying my hospitality no less ... well, impolite things would happen that I'd rather not dwell upon. So hush, Louis. Silence is golden.

May I have a little nod, Louis, to signal your understanding?

Splendid! Thank you Louis. You are a gentleman always. And now, may I have your promise?

Wonderful! I'm so relieved. You're a wise man, Louis, and a master of subtlety. Now I shall attend to you. I'll bring scissors to cut away that gag, a bandage for that gash, and an antiseptic for those cuts on your face. And, since waiting is our project, I believe I can find us more comfortable chairs, and a cloth for this sticky table. A candle or two will improve the lighting, and I don't know about you Louis but a glass of something Bandol would sure soothe my nerves. How about it? I have an '09 Tempier that's begging to be opened. Would you like a sip?

Excellent! Oh Louis, if you could see your face light up! I do like a man with appetites.

So, I'll fetch all that, and two glasses, and then, Louis, to elevate our wait and support our patience, and to give you the fortification you clearly need, it will be my delight and honor to serve Louis De Gustibus, the great gourmand and critic, a simple dinner à l'Arche! A meal of the type that's recently made us so popular with the elites. Since we are unexpectedly closed today, my kitchen is stocked and hot, and I abhor the waste of food ...

Louis: you've gone pale as octopus. Even the blood vessels in your nose have blanched. What's the problem? Isn't this why you tracked me down, you big bloodhound? Despite our best and until now successful efforts at disappearance? I'm still dying to know who told you, Louis. Did your magazine put you up to this, or is it just one of your solo missions?

But there will be time for questions and answers. Stories, conversation, philosophy and good food—it's what men like us live for. I'm giddy with excitement, Louis! I just can't wait.

Look at my eyes, Louis! Look at me! Yes, the windows of your soul are flung wide open—I see you in there, building a wall between us. You're thinking: I will refuse. You're thinking: I would rather die. You're calling me names: cannibal, monster, madman.

Touché, Louis. You scratch my heart.

But ... it's understandable. You don't trust me yet. Too much tumult, too much trauma. But I will earn your trust. If we're going to escape this sticky situation topside with our skins on, I'll

19

need it. And I know you'll judge me, Louis. You are the foremost measure of my art; all chefs live to be judged by you. I only ask that you first know me. You've got to let me explain.

Eating millionaires is not wrong, Louis. It's not even amoral. Eating millionaires is good, the greatest good I've managed to accomplish in my cruelly compromised career. In fact, I believe it's imperative we eat them all. I've thought long and hard on this; I am married to the notion. So tonight, over a relaxing dinner, I invite you to critique both my cooking and my philosophy. It needn't be brutal, Louis, but one of us will change his mind.

And in fact I have a surprise for you, Louis. Something I can't wait to show you! Louis, if I still believed in God I would kneel down on this scummy floor and thank him for delivering you to me!

But fear not. I'm no apocalyptic ranter; rational discourse is all I ask—that and your good company! I've read all of your work, Louis—in fact I became wholly obsessed with your review during our first encounter at l'Aubergine—and I know you to be erudite, broad-minded, appreciative of all delicacy, fair but firm. Your salute to Monsieur Pratt of l'Equinox was stirring and well-deserved; I only wish he could have read it in his lifetime. Your exposé of those frauds at Spice Nine was cruel, perhaps, but long overdue in my opinion. And effective, too; if anyone ever doubted that your pen is the sword on which inferior restaurants are impaled, they sure believe it now. Why, who could forget that controversial episode at La Tartine, when was it, seven years ago? Your career, you know, has always overhung my own: me at the food processor, you at the word processor, both of us tracing the same arc: to know the best, to give every ingredient its due, to taste the world and everything in it.

So now, on the eve of my retirement, at the pinnacle of my career, in the hour of my greatest need, you are here! I take back what I said about your timing, Louis: it couldn't be better. Just let me fetch the right bottle of wine, and then you and I will share a perfect meal and have a splendidly civilized chat about the eating of millionaires.

Sorry for the wait. I hope the rats didn't tickle you too much—
they're curious creatures, but they rarely bite.

I would have come sooner but Marko is having one of his
episodes—in my kitchen no less! Did you hear the clattering?
He's throwing pans around, overturning the stock pots, stabbing
the knives into the countertops, making a Marko-sized mess. I
didn't dare approach; he is a bit of a stabber, our Marko. In fact,

I'd say he lives to stab. Stabbing seems to speak to something in his soul; he often stands in front of the knife cabinet, feeling the heft of each knife, slowly turning them in his hand and then— stab! He jabs snakelike at the air, or the table, or the body of whomever he might be in the process of killing. I've even watched him stab himself, in the palm of his own left hand, just to feel the sharpness. I will not get within ten feet of Marko while he's holding a knife.

But as I said, it's just an episode; once he gets the stabbing out of his system he's much more reasonable. I know him well. So I let him be busy with that while I snuck circuitously to the wine cellar, and I have returned with the implement we need, see? The waiter's friend, from Laguiole. Our sommelier, Salome, left it in her bib in the break room. She won't be back for it.

Now please hold still. It's a tiny blade, but very sharp, and I wouldn't want to nick your neck. It's sterling silver, you know, like all our tableware and much of our cutlery. Our customers notice such things, find it ostentatious in the best way, but in truth silver gives us the upper hand in the war against corrosion.

Operating a restaurant on this old boat: I tell you, it's two full jobs. Even moored in this calm lagoon we suffer in storms, we're jerked around by wind and tides, screaming sea birds shit on us, and the sea air is full of rust.

Also, the noise! The ever-present clatter echoing through the hull can be maddening. That regular mechanical cough and sputter you hear is our palpitating bilge pump; it keeps us afloat as we take in water from a hundred tiny holes. That deep rumbling buzz is our diesel generator; it powers these flickering lights, the squealing refrigeration pumps and the staticky radios and the whining ventilation fans, all of them surging up and down as the waves slap us around and the diesel sloshes in the bottom of the tank. So much noise! It used to wear at my nerves, at first. Now, of course, I find I've become nearly deaf to it. It is amazing what one can get used to.

All these rats, for instance. What chef or captain has ever been free of them? Any other restaurateur would lay traps, or poison, or release vipers. Alas, Louis, I cannot; you know how I am. I only kill what I eat. I shoo them away, or lose my temper and storm after them, but still they peer at me from the crevices, twitching, combing their whiskers, observing ... my little gray witnesses. You know how I admire animals of every kind. Rats are such civilized creatures, Louis. They're greedy, but they won't cross certain lines. I believe they know which side their bread is buttered on.

Also, they're terrified of Marko; that keeps them out of the dining room. Our kitchen is scrupulously clean when Marko isn't ravaging it, so they usually don't hang around there. Mainly they live down here, in the belly of the boat, nibbling on abattoir scraps. They have refined tastes, our rats. They love millionaires as much as I do—

Oh dear! Your neck: I went and nicked it. Christ. I beg your pardon, Louis. Please don't squirm, I'm almost done. It's just a tiny gash, we'll touch it up with a styptic pencil, as soon as Marko moves away from the medical kit.

Here we are ... voilà! Spit out that gauze, spit it all out! You're free at last!

Say something, Louis, but—quietly! Remember your promise. Whisper to me: how do you feel? What do you need? Tell me anything.

Louis?

Oh, forgive me! You're parched, seated at a table with a cold bottle of Domaine Tempier directly before you, and here I am with a corkscrew in my hand and a thumb up my ass. Say no more. Château Laguiole to the rescue, again.

Do you know, Salome informed me recently that rats have been nibbling on the corks in our cellar! And they seem to know a thing or two about wine—they were drawn to Veuve Clicquot and the Châteauneufs. But they've turned up their noses at this one ... it's a clean cork. I'll let you be the judge.

Salome, you know, was a fair young woman of surprising taste and voracious knowledge, and she stocked the best. Observe it in the glass: the body, the legs, the color. A promising start.

Now if you'll allow me, I'll very gently hold this glass below your nose, as your hands are tied—now breathe. Inhale the bouquet. Simple and sweet, yes? A lovely young wine. Of course you can't warm it in your hands until I undo your wrists—yes, I intend to! Yes! It's all coming, but ... we really ought to have a drink first. Let's start there.

Breathe it in, Louis. Yes? And just a taste?

Ahhh ... that is some praise. That is some thirst! That is an appetite. There's so much going on in this glass. Do you feel the Muschelkalk on your teeth? Cherries, musty earth ... the flavor is bottomless. It's a wine you can dive into.

My dear Louis, I'm so glad you're here. It's so good to trace that familiar pathway to your heart. Let me pour a toast: to hospitality, damn the weather! To old friendship, renewed. And to absent, brilliant Salome. Yes?

Mmm ... Salome would blush. You flatter her, Louis, but I

agree it's good stuff. I'd let it open up a bit first, but ... more? Well, all right. There you go, my friend, with gusto. But please be careful not to dull you senses. It's a very special night; there's so much more for you to taste.

I'm curious, Louis: how long have you been with us, docked on the isle of Cristobal Minor? Have you even been ashore yet? Have you walked up the planks, passed that tin roofed guardhouse and the comical yellow stripe that marks the edge of international waters? Have you visited our hosts, the modest citizens of Cristobal Minor? Have you sampled the native crafts?

Or did you only just today emerge from the belly of whichever yacht you rode in on? Yes, judging from your paleness, your lack of a wealthy tan, the crispness of your pleats, I'd say you've just arrived.

But Louis: you must visit the island! That is, I hope you'll get the opportunity. It is a beautiful place; up until just recently I would have also called the Cristobos a very welcoming people.

Cristobal Minor is a charming, charming little micro-nation, free as the wind and entirely alone out here in the great big sea, hundreds of kilometers from anything so tedious as a police force, a tax collector or a continent—a Libertarian utopia. This little bay is so placid in the summer months, the water such a remarkable shade of blue, and when the sun sets directly behind that volcanic mound at the center of the island it is the stuff of postcards. The hand-hewn planks of the pier, dilapidated as they are, lend the whole enterprise such an authentic glow of roughness, scrappiness, island-ness. The millionaires just lap it up. It's a theme park for them, a Disneyland of poverty.

Poverty, yes. Cristobal Minor is poor, poor, poor! A tiny population supported by a sad little fleet of fishing boats, they have scraped by for a few hundred years under astonishingly bad conditions. In the stormy season, the entire island is regularly flooded. The topsoil is clogged with salt. All their tools for survival are imported on their fishing boats—leaky desperate things that regularly sink, taking entire families down at once. The only resource these thin, bent-over, inbred, struggling little people have ever had was a certain regular influx of fresh seafood, and subsisting on that they've clung, proudly, to this adorable pimple on the back of the ocean.

But you know. You're aware, a man of your times, not one of those ostrich-headed deniers of bad news. The sea is not such a lovely young woman any more. Humanity has ridden her hard and given her diseases, and she's bitter about it. In this region, the proud industrial fishing fleets of many nations used to deplete the sea of metric tons of sea life every calm day. But they don't come here any more. The fish are all gone, eaten up on land. Dip a hook in these waters now and you'd best be very careful with what you reel in.

Overfishing is one culprit, the same old story told over and over in different seas. Those industrial fishermen loved the ocean, truly; they saw, in her, eternal youth and bottomless fortune. L'Arche, this very ship of ours, used to be one such boat: a purse seiner with Indonesian flags. She worked these very waters, and others close by. Each morning the captain would inscribe a ten kilometer circle on the surface of the ocean, lay down a floating net one thousand fathoms deep, then tightly cinch shut the bottom of the net like an upside-down coin purse—hence the name "purse seine"—thereby netting several hundred billion gallons of the living ocean in one bold scoop. The crew spent the rest of the day winching aboard and hacking apart every living thing within that doomed circumference. Tons and tons of fish, Louis, of every kind. Tuna mainly, but also swordfish, flying fish, dolphins, jellyfish, whales, giant squid—I dare say if mermaids ever existed, l'Arche caught one. And those fishermen, well, I doubt they would have released her from that net without first checking her market price.

And like all great industrial projects, this went swimmingly until it didn't. But by the time the local tuna population—and by extension the population of Cristobal Minor—began to collapse, another problem was advancing: pollution. Floating plastic trash—microscopic bits of bags, water bottles, wrappers, tchotchkes, garbage of all kinds. Because we are only a few hundred kilometers, Louis, from a most astonishing sargasso sea of floating plastic trash. It has been growing steadily for twenty years at least and is still growing, faster today than ever.

I've had an occasion to boat out there, with Marko, to collect ingredients from some skittish gentlemen who wished to remain a certain distance from any sort of sovereign nation, for purely personal reasons. They hide their yacht in this trash pile; it disguises them beautifully from above. It's astounding there. You can't even see the water, just a mildly undulating landscape of glistening, fluttering garbage. Peer deeply into it and you begin to recognize your own history. That cork, that wrapper, that bottle of filtered water: did I consume those? Did I throw my trash in the sea, or did it blow there after I left it on the ground? Is that floating sandal the one I lost on my visit to Tahiti? That brightly colored sand bucket: didn't I have one just like it when I was a child? Was I guilty even then? Was I already engineering the downfall of the hardscrabble citizens of Cristobal Minor?

Now, imagine yourself in the position of the Cristobos. The sea, which has always grudgingly provided, appears to be finished with you. The nets of the fishermen are bringing up only juice cartons and hairbrushes and mud. Given your desperation you might consider eating the hairbrushes, but soon you realize: your way of life is finished. You must abandon your island, leave it or die. You had almost nothing, but now you have even less. You stare out over the frothing ocean and fret; you huddle with your hare-lipped children and weep.

But then—imagine, the very next day or a day soon after, a strange man arrives on a mighty ship. He is immense, silent, coiffed in the trappings of exquisite wealth, serious and impressive ... in other words, imagine that Marko shows up on your island in your moment of greatest need, bringing with him a supply of meat and some of the magical paper money that sailors can trade for things in far away ports. And Marko explains to you in his hypnotizing voice that all is not lost, there is still one thing you own, one thing you can sell ... and that is your freedom.

The story of Cristobal Minor's nationhood is curious, slightly ridiculous. About two hundred years ago it was claimed for strategic reasons by Argentine admirals. They shipped a dubious set of paupers here: displaced Mapuche indians, refugees from other conquered islands, plus a smattering of European criminals, accompanied by rabbits and pigs and dogs. They were dropped off with little more than a wave and the promise of a new bustling port and all the prosperity that might come with it. But that seed never sprouted; the schemers of this plan had mis-measured the winds, prevailing currents and overall reachability of the place. So the immigrants sat here, forgotten, for some time under the Argentine flag. Their first year was hard: the rabbits quickly eradicated what little indigenous flora existed, then the dogs ate the rabbits, then the men ate the pigs and the dogs, then they began to eat one another. Eventually they learned to fish.

But one day, unmarked by anyone here, the Argentines grew weary of owning this island and its inhabitants who seemed always to be appealing to their government for aid. So the magnanimous parent country did what birds do to their offspring: it pushed Cristobal Minor out of the nest. In a pitched ceremony onboard a visiting gunboat, this island was granted self-determination, wished good luck and good riddance. An orphaned island in a rough sea, it has longed ever since to be declared useful and invaded anew.

Long story short: Marko saved this island. Rescued it. He cleaned it up, made it pretty, put it to work. Cristobal Minor, once a humanitarian disaster, is now a *destination*. It's a place for yachtsmen to yacht to, and yachtsmen need such places; the very difficulty of reaching this island makes landing here a trophy pursuit. Once moored, they might visit the tiny beach, where market forces have called into existence a slapdash but cheerful main drag for Cristobos to hawk their freshly adopted native crafts and perform recently composed traditional music. Or else the millionaires can sit on the decks of their mighty yachts, watching the sun set on the amazing blue water. admiring one another's pleasure craft.

They may swim, too ... if their yachts are equipped with pools. Alas, swimming in the lagoon itself is not recommended, not in the least. Pollution, you know, is what tints the water so sparkling. Microscopic plastic shards glinting in the sun, a pound of invisible crap in every gallon. It leaves a bit of a disagreeable slime on one, although it also waxes the hulls of the ships, which I'm told makes them faster. And the sea life that still survives in this undead lagoon, well ... if you need proof that the ocean is angry with humankind, just try swimming to shore from this boat. The water is thick with the deadly box jellyfish known as the Sea Wasp. Dozens of them will swarm on you, paralyzing you with agonizing toxins from their tendrils. If the pain alone doesn't kill you, you'll feel your heart stop, your skin swell and burst. Then a local population of sickly deformed eels will nip away your flesh, and a host of tiny black crabs will pick your bones clean with remarkable efficiency.

Still, in lieu of swimming we have sunbathing, shopping, snapshots, the aforementioned native crafts, yacht racing in the plastic-lubricated waters, et cetera. All day long, so much for a millionaire to do. But when night falls, there is only one thing: l'Arche! This restaurant—my restaurant—is the anchor of the entire project. This is what draws the millionaires: my food! My knowledge, my senses, my skill, the unclassifiable essence of my soul that I pour into every dish.

And, yes, the select ingredients.

But now ... who knows what the future holds for the cursed population of Cristobal Minor? One thing is certain: we are done here. Our welcome has expired.

Did you hear those gunshots? It's hard, I know, to pick out sounds through the wind and rain and noise, but I think I heard

Marko firing at the shore. There's a surly phalanx of Cristobos still down there, hiding behind that tin guard house, gathering their numbers, sharpening their axes, chanting epithets in that unique Spanish pidgin of theirs. I think they're waiting for an opening, a chance to storm us. But don't worry; he won't give them one. He's an exquisite shot, our Marko.

Still, I'd best check in with the overall situation; then I will return with our first course. Here's another sip of wine to hold you. I promise I won't be long.

Voilà! Look alive, Louis! I present the charcuterie plate: Gallantine of Millionaire, Millionaire Andouillette, Millionaire Zampino, Millionaire Boudin Blanc, Millionaire Boudin Noir, dry-cured prosciutto of millionaire, and a hot baby giraffe salami. Various patés, yesterday's bread. In the dining room we present this on a long slender tray, arranged in reference to Zallinger's March of Progress, but given how this storm is smacking us against the piers I thought a basket would be safer. If a slice of this sausage were to fall off the table, I guarantee a rat would intercept it not halfway to the floor. It's better we don't encourage them; they need to know their place.

Marko upstairs is enjoying the same first course, sans giraffe. Actually we've both been hitting the giraffe rather hard; Marko reached his limit last week. It's quite a bit less digestible than millionaires, but tasty, and variety is the spice, you know. And we've got a hell of a lot of this particular spice, giraffes being enormous and millionaires capricious.

He has curious hunger, our Marko. He demands food at the oddest moments, and won't be satisfied to wait. Even now, as we pitch and heave in this storm—shame about the wine, I'll fetch another bottle—right now Marko is seated in his wheelhouse throne, firing one-handed out the window, while with his other hand he's feeding himself dainty bites of sausage with a silver fondue fork. He's such an oddball. But I love to feed a hungry man, Louis. It fills me with joy, watching him grow strong on our millionaires.

Do you know that when I first studied sausage-making at Le Coup Amiable, I was still a vegetarian self-declared! Imagine: blood on my kind hands every day, grease and gore up to my gentle elbows, on my caring shoes, in my innocent eyes ... I intended the job as a penance, in fact, for my failure to feed the masses. But then, under the tutelage of Chef M. Delacroix, I really took wing. Charcuterie became my first speciality, and butchery my second. Meat, bone, blood, the still-warm insides of animals: there is something beautiful in that, a glimpse of the miraculous. I just couldn't maintain my disgust. I tell you, to slip your arm into the soft cavity of a just-killed millionaire, wriggle past the air-filled stomach, caress the lungs, trace the inter-connective tissues, feel the hotness of the just-stopped heart ... I find it strangely sensual, Louis. Sometimes when I'm breaking down a millionaire I close my eyes and imagine I am caressing perfect Nature herself.

Sausage is also, I think, the easiest introduction to the taste of millionaires because it's so transformed; it is the most abstract form of meat. Traditionally, it's also the most lied about. Sausage can be anything you want it to be; only the butcher knows for sure. I could tell you this is actually mutton, or pork, or textured vegetable protein. Or even giraffe. Would you try it then? Smell it, Louis.

But no, not you—you'd know the difference instantly! Famous Gourmet Louis De Gustibus, with your incorruptible tongue, your heroic palate, your pendulous nose that sniffs out all deceivers. Just look at you: your big eyes unblinking, your senses sharpened by the plate before you. You're breathing faster—your nostrils are fluttering, Louis! Your great elephant's ears are pricking up! No, I'd never dare slip millionaires into your tofu, Louis. Not even for your own good.

So, speaking of: which will you try first? The Boudin Blanc is my favorite; it really highlights the delicate qualities of millionaires' blood. But perhaps the Zampino is more tempting to an Italophile?

Charcuterie is the art of preservation, of course: every item on this plate arrived fresh one month ago, by yacht. I won't soon forget the moment. It was late morning, a Cristobo waiter named Raoul and I were dumping a bucket of indigestibles over the leeward side, when the asinine scion of some spreadsheet fortune, fresh from Namibia, pulled alongside us on his bright red double-engined landing vessel—dispatched from the belly of a larger service vessel, that in turn follows his father's truly gargantuan luxury liner all around the globe—and deposited this poorly-bled, poorly-iced and shotgun-perforated beast onto our decks—one thousand pounds of unrefrigerated baby giraffe dropped from a crane like an immense spotted bony birdshit without so much as an "are you open?"—and instructed us to drop whatever else we were doing to get it ready for a late supper that evening for his friends. How many friends? What time? Not sure, he said, but save the skin, it's valuable. And he adjusted his ludicrous sailor's cap and motored away in a spray of salt water and hundred dollar bills.

Now that is the kind of millionaire I like to eat.

And that is the kind of millionaire we serve here at our humble bistro l'Arche: nouveau-rich gadabouts returning from chartered safaris with something they've killed. They're drawn to us like calamari to the lamps of a fishing boat, and with them they bring lions, apes, pandas, eagles, elephants and more. They come to pay reverence to our motto: Consume Quod Interficis.

(Come now, Louis, don't make faces. You've really got to try some of this. Andouillette? Blood sausage? Just say the word.)

But just how do they find us? L'Arche does not advertise. Bien au contraire, we suppress the very fact of our existence in every way we can. We have no sign, no website, no Michelin stars. We require contracts of confidentiality from our guests, but that secrecy, that discretion ... it somehow attaches to millionaires like pheromones to the feelers of ants, and is transmitted, millionaire to millionaire, throughout their quiet global network, until we have become the most exclusive and desirable dinner location ever to not exist. No one has spoken, but everyone knows. Although our diners daily violate international laws for the preservation of wildlife and there's not a customer we couldn't blackmail, still they can't stay away. I don't mean to brag, Louis, but what other chef inspires such loyalty?

(Now Louis ... open your mouth, won't you? You'll thank me later. The texture of this Boudin Noir, I guarantee it's the best you've had.)

Our unique operating bargain is this: we cook *everything*. Anything you can provide we will prepare, with the best science of Escoffier, deliciously and discreetly. Endangered species are a speciality, of course, and so we initially drew customers from the modern safari circuit who, having bagged a lion in an African game preserve, could find no one else qualified to cook it. But our recent boom has been fed by a different sort of customer, one who simply develops an inexplicable craving one day for, say, orangutan, and subcontracts the details.

The most charming feature of millionaires is that they love to do the impossible. They especially savor any experience which they know to be exclusive, unavailable to most. They are constantly trying to out-impossiblize one another. For our earliest customers, dinner at l'Arche represented a coup of the impossible. But for this current crowd it's just the newest option, a way to keep up with the Rockefellers, to prove that they, too, can afford the latest impossible thing. Millionaires need to convince themselves, constantly, that they are still millionaires. They are always pinching themselves to see if they are dreaming.

(Speaking of pinching: I wonder, if I very gently squeeze your nostrils shut like so, if that won't part your lips soon enough for a taste of Zampino ...)

Truth is, the millionaires have suffered some rude awakenings this year. You've read the news, of course, you've heard the hand-wringing politicians explain the joys of austerity and the pointlessness of blame. You've seen, I'm sure, the growing throngs of hungry men on the street, or rioting outside the bank towers, smashing one another against the glass, demanding money that seems to have escaped out the back. Even here on this insignificant little island of Cristobal Minor where the natives live on nearly nothing, their portions of nothing have shrunk by half. Our own business is booming—was booming, until today—and that brought a certain economic stimulus that the locals once appreciated—they certainly *seemed* to—but in all our dealings with the outside world we still see everywhere the wreckage of this unprecedented, inexplicable disease that seems to have infected the world's money.

But if you think the poor have it rough, you should see how it's affected our millionaires! Have you noticed? Some large and complex machinery that only they understand, some component of the financial engine that levitates the few above the heads of the many, quietly exploded last year. Markets shuddered, banks collapsed, hunks of flaming debt are still falling from the sky.

All this makes the millionaires very tense. It's in their eyes: they seem almost afraid to look up. When they laugh it's with nervous, forced laughter. When they fight it's with deep-rooted panic and naked aggression. Their consumption, always conspicuous, has grown ridiculous—they've never had more to prove to one another, it seems! And whereas I once observed them to maintain a laudable fraternity of class, lately many of our guests exude a subtle paranoia, a mutual mistrust of one another in close quarters.

(Oh Louis, don't make faces. You can't hold your breath forever.)

Perhaps it's the killings. Killing one another seems to be their latest distraction. An elegant form of internecine warfare has become popular among the rich. They're armoring their yachts, fitting them with extravagant cannons. They are arriving at l'Arche under heavier security, with larger and more numerous bodyguards, and their spring fashion is for hand-tooled leather holsters and designer bandoliers.

In fact one of our regular patrons, a Mr. Hazmat, is an arms dealer—at least, I call him that; he has some tidier name for it— who specializes in those upmarket paramilitary accessories. He's done quite a few deals over dinner at l'Arche; this is where his target market dines. And he, like us, is having a banner year.

(Aha! In we go! Now chew, Louis. No spitting ... rub it against your teeth, feel the texture ... that's right ... detect the fennel, the cracked charnushka ... is that so awful, Louis? I thought not. Now swallow ...)

There is a growing festival of feuds, now, among the millionaires. Every day new scores to be settled. Feuds over assets, of course, but also over status, pride, betrayal. I only hear whispers—I am but a humble chef at the service of wealth, and I am ever discreet—but I gather that in recent years preceding this unprecedented money fiasco, the rich have been intimately defrauding one another in various ways too complex for any of them to understand. And this only became suddenly apparent last year when, to hear them tell it, large sums of money began to disappear all over the world. Or, rather, various things that had looked like money turned out not to be money, and people who thought they held money were found to hold descriptions of money, paintings of money, empty promises of future money, farewell notes from money departed. Suddenly every millionaire became simultaneously curious about every other millionaire's money and utterly secretive regarding their own. Now nobody is really certain who has money and who doesn't, but everyone has a theory about the blame.

Some months back I had an interesting chat with a charming millionaire who posited, over a butter-braised polar bear paw and a second bottle of Riesling, that the world's rich had been milking one another like an interconnected system of cows for over a decade, without once pausing to ingest any grass. This man called for a great reckoning, a final audit of who owns what and who owes who, and while he didn't say as much, I imagine his accounting practices were coarser than yours or mine. He seemed to relish the coming struggle: a chance to test his new guns. Millionaires do, I've found, enjoy a good struggle, especially when they spot an advantage in the rules.

Curiously, that same millionaire was delivered to our service entrance just a few days later, packed in ice and stripped of belongings—the trophy of another, larger millionaire. (It was in fact Mr. Hazmat who killed him. I have no idea why; I never ask.) He had more than a few holes in him; we found sea water in his lungs and bruises all up and down his spine, but his liver was delicate and soft. I like to think we did him justice. It's hard to go wrong with millionaires.

(But please, do also try the giraffe.)

So the rich yachtsmen, in short, are killing one another out here in the international waters they adore. They're doing it out of spite, or for vengeance, or just as another way of being rich. They like to get away with murder; it confirms their status. But then, having gotten away with that, they are still at pains to delete the evidence. They are detail-oriented, our overlords. My business partner, Marko, who has a certain genius in his dealing with the millionaires, offers them discreet assistance with just this sort of problem, and I in turn offer them an unparalleled opportunity to savor ultimate victory.

That, in a nutshell, is how we got started in millionaires. It was never really part of the business plan, but then again, once we advertised our willingness to cook anything—any goddamn thing—it was only a matter of time before they took us up on the offer.

So, Louis: what do you make of it? The texture, the aroma, the way the fat glistens in the candlelight ... what does it say to you? Some have compared it to bacon. I find it very different. But for you, Louis, arbiter of flavor, what reaction does it provoke? What fireworks are lit in your capacious head? What language is unspooling? Please, tell me what you're thinking. Feed me some of your delicious words, Louis. Be honest.

Where is your tongue, Louis? You haven't spoken one syllable since you arrived. Have you sworn an acetic vow?

Or are you overwhelmed by the progress of events? I

sympathize. I won't press you, of course, but I will warn you: the alternative is for me to prattle on and on like this.

You do hear me, don't you? You will have another sip of wine, won't you? Yes, I see we are communicating on at least that level. With you so tied up and silent, I'm put in mind of a mother with her swaddled infant. Such a strange position for me, Louis, as I have always considered you the elder, the authority, the man I looked up to. Not a father, not nearly ... but then again perhaps you are the closest thing.

I have no parents that I know of. As a sickly infant I was deposited in a shoddy little orphanage, l'Ophelinat Saint Antoine De Padoue, in Grenoble—a great gray bunker of a place. The nuns of the order raised me: tired shrews, obsessed with sacrifice and obedience. They claimed to love us unwanted boys, and what affection they had they did distribute equally and interchangeably, like workers on the factory line. As much as I or another boy might have dreamed of a personal nun to call mother, such attachments were not allowed on the premises. We were the motherless, the rejected and wretched, yet expected to be thankful—all part of God's plan, you see.

The priests, of course, were far too familiar—I won't scandalize you with details. Obedience, silence, and various acts called "love". In the aftermath of such encounters, I was often advised to accept Jesus as my supreme parent, and look to Him for explanation. But Jesus wasn't around much—not when I needed him most. As deeply as I longed to, I'm afraid I never got to know the man.

Still, Catholicism clings to one's feet like dogshit. Even though I have no use for children's stories about Jesus, still, there is something about this crucified gentleman here on the wall, the same one who watched over all my childhood tortures, that I find comforting. Look at him hanging on that cross like a dry-cured ham, a portrait of pain and doom, but he does not resist. Eat me, he says; taste my body, drink my blood. Know me, consume me, and be saved. *That,* I say, is true hospitality.

And when we invite live millionaires down here to be stuck and bled, they find that crucifix captivating, perhaps soothing. Often they burst out in prayer. But they don't imitate Christ. There are no tortures, no crown of thorns. We do the deed quickly and humanely, under the merciful eyes of Christ Our Meat Inspector, the one man who's seen it all.

At any rate, if I go overboard in my manic desire to please you, Louis, please forgive me, as Jesus would. If hospitality is my calling, then you are my shining light.

Now you *must* taste the Andouillette, it's my signature sausage. Open wide ...

Taste: it is a burden, don't you agree? Doesn't it simply interfere with living? To the man of taste, most things taste *terrible*. The tasteful man, the true gourmet, regularly finds coffee stale, vegetables soggy and bland, meat dry, odors alarming and spoons unclean. To have standards is to be always rejecting things. It's a paradox that weighs heavy on my profession.

The pursuit of the best, the freshest, the healthiest and most delicious ... it ought to be adventure, strenuous fun with a noble reward, but sometimes it's an anxious march up a steep incline. One is lured, yes, by the aromas of rarer and more precious delights, yes, but also one is driven upward, repelled by the nauseating ocean of everything else, that great stinking tide of the substandard that only ever seems to rise: stale food, fast food, plastic food, gas-ripened, steroid-injected, nuclear-irradiated industrial food.

And as our man of taste ascends this mountain, higher and higher, the sights grow splendid indeed, but paradoxically there is less and less for him to eat. So many things just won't do, just don't please, just aren't right. The search for new flavors, tastes and experiences devolves from a vivacious curiosity to a morbid, consuming need, until finally, our mountaineer reaches the rarefied peak, beholds the exquisite vista, tastes what is unquestionably the best of everything—and even this is just not good enough. It leaves him cold.

One becomes jaded. It happened to me. It happens to all of us to a degree. An occupational hazard. Are you immune, Louis? I doubt it.

It fairly plagues our guests, this condition—after all, l'Arche is positioned on a certain apex of this Ararat. We are the best of something, certainly, and the only source of many things. Plus, millionaires are particularly susceptible to this degeneracy, insomuch as they can hire whole teams of Sherpas to haul them up that poisoned mountain without exerting themselves in the least.

Fortunately for you and I, nature has provided a complimentary sense to the man of taste: an ethical sense, a sense not of what one might fancy but of what one must do! We know it is wrong to turn up our noses at a meal while others go hungry. And so we shut up, drink our bitter coffee, eat our soggy vegetables and count ourselves lucky to be fed at all! Moreover, ethics compel us to share our meals with our friends, with strangers, even with our enemy if he's truly in need. It's the golden rule, this sense of empathy, this ability to see ourselves in others. That rule is, I think, the very core of hospitality itself. One wants not just to eat, but to serve. Not just to be happy, but to entertain. It's that sense of knowing that we are all more or less the same.

It is a sense I have noticed grievously absent in certain millionaires. Perhaps that's natural: perhaps they're not at all the same as us. The millionaire's relationship to the whole of humanity seems very different from yours and mine, very much more complicated. They need us, yes, and perhaps we need them—certainly Marko has uses for them—but that need is always so awkward. Because they take, Louis, so much more than they give. By definition. And everybody knows it.

Their lack of ethics, I think, is the key to their success. The problem of ethics is symmetrical with the trouble of taste: the more we aspire to goodness, the more we find evil all around us, and inside us too. As much as we cook, people still starve. As good as we can be, we could always be better. But the better we become, the harder it is to endure the bad, tasteless world.

Eventually one must take up the mortifications of sainthood: reject violence, renounce wealth, all that. One can give up so much in the name of good—factory farmed meat, processed sugar, unjustly harvested grapes—but I've observed that it's never the needy who wind up with the resulting surplus. It's always the millionaires.

As a child I had wealth renounced for me, but then later, in my twenties, when I had finally gone to school and got a job and gained a bit of wealth, I renounced it again, right away. I gave away my knives and my books, I lived in the street, so greatly did I feel the need to share. I was that good!

I was once so good, Louis, that every day under a bridge on the Seine out beyond the Périphérique I conjured a Consommé—Mock Oxtail Soup, I called it—of boiled down scraps from kitchens where I still had friends or knew schedules, along with gleanings from the markets. I served this, daily, to an endless line of poor immigrants, addicts, the chronically unlucky and the unhospitalized insane. In the name of Saint Anthony, I declared, I would feed the starving! I still had a head full of Catholic mess; for what those old molesters at the orphanage did to me, *I* felt an urgent need to *atone*.

That was my first restaurant: battered pots over smoldering bits of wood, chipped bowls, mismatched spoons, slime dripping from the overpass. And I met smashing success: the lines of hungry losers grew longer every day. But hungry they stayed, Louis. There was never enough stew for them. I worked harder, I procured more, I deputized others to find ingredients. Hungry, desperate men brought stolen beef, rotten cabbages from the trash bins, crushed eggshells, animals killed by cars. Everything went in the stew—through hungry eyes it all looked so wholesome!—but it was still not enough. The hordes were all so bony and desperate, and more of them arrived every day, an army of hunger, teeth and tongues outstretched. Hunger clung to these people's faces, infested their bodies, spread through their population. I wielded the intoxicating power to soothe them with a touch of my soup ladle, but only for a while. Hunger always retreats, regroups, returns redoubled.

Oh, the things I gave away in my journey up the mountain called Good: my coat, my shoes, my dry spot under the bridge, my sanity. And one day I reached the peak: I was as good as I will ever get. I had nothing, nothing at all. I was weak, delirious. I gave everything. But, as good as I was, I found myself twice as hungry. And the lines never ceased.

Let me tell you, Louis: there's no bistro at the top of that mountain. You can't eat goodness. You can't drink righteousness. You can either starve to death self-satisfied, or else you can climb back down for lunch. As it happened, I was forced to leave after an argument with a local health bureaucrat, but that was just an excuse. In truth, I gave up. I conceded the territory to hunger.

Food is life, yes, but also: food is death. It's life eating life. Others must die so that we may live; there's never enough food for everybody. The decision to live is the decision to kill. The rest is boring details that animals don't bother with: vegetarianism, veganism, localism, ethical practices, kosherness, organicness—who shall we kill, in other words, and how shall we kill them? Those are the highest values that we may aspire to, we who have decided to live.

I did try to be a vegetarian once, but vegetarians no longer impress me. They never wonder where their fields come from, or who had to be removed to make room for the plow. They have no sense of history. Show me a farm, and I'll show you a battlefield. Vegetarians fetishize inaction, as I once did. They can brag about the evils they don't do, but what is the good they do instead?

And the good I do? I assuage hunger, same as always. It's my life's work. In a more general sense I alleviate suffering, as best I can. But what way is best? Which suffering? I can't alleviate it all, can I? And I would forgive any principled soul who suggested that feeding the best foods to the most well-fed individuals is not the way to make a dent in humanity's reserves of suffering. Obviously. The millionaires, they do not suffer. Yes they do on occasion have *problems*—loneliness, infidelity, deceased pets— but generally the millionaires delegate their actual *suffering* to others. A great deal of human suffering is, in fact, the misplaced suffering of millionaires.

Here at l'Arche we return their lost suffering to them. We help them to understand how the other half hurts. That is but one of the many elite services we provide.

I don't mean to alarm you, Louis, but have you noticed this water on the floor? Our four-legged friends have; they're scampering to higher ground. That is something the bilge pumps ought to be purging for us. It's curious. Not to worry, but I'd better have a look-see.

Plus, Marko will be wanting his next course, as will we ours. Barring any more mayhem in the kitchen the main courses ought to be rested and ready by now. So excuse me once again; I'll be back in a flash. If the rats get nippy with you, just scream at them. They're toothy little beasts but they do respect authority.

Good news, Louis: we're sinking! You've probably guessed as much—my, how the bloody brine sloshes. I do apologize for the dankness of it all. Given our circumstances, a little sea-water in the socks is insult to injury. But I assure you we're on the high side of the problem. In the engine room things are much, much worse. The bilge pumps are slooshing and groaning desperately, but all this grating against the piers has opened up not one but I believe several leaks in the port side of our old hull. With luck we'll be underwater in a matter of hours.

The forces! Gravity, wind and water, buoyancy and diesel,

ammunition, money and Marko. Their dance is accelerating, Louis. Soon we'll cut in. This sinking is particularly encouraging to me because I half expected Marko to try an escape by sea, when and if this storm ever starts to lift. On this old boat we'd stand no chance. It barely floats at dockside, the engines are ancient rattling things, the leaking tanks can't be filled more than halfway with fuel, and the linkage between wheel and rudder is more of a mutual acquaintance than any kind of dependable relationship.

Consider also that my kitchen is barely able to weather these dockside swells. If we got on the high seas I'm sure my pantry would be scattered throughout the ship, the dining room furniture would fly through the glass and over the rails ... not that it would matter, not now, but I would prefer a more dignified ending.

Our walk-in cooler, however, is situated in the safest zone of the hull, up one deck from here, just below the kitchen, centered over the keel. After this course, we'll relocate. You'll find it cold, but calm. The meat hangs from hooks, so a bit of side-to-side is no worry at all. The room's insulation ought to afford us a bit more privacy, and I can show you my millionaire collection.

At any rate, escape by sea is clearly out of the question now, and Marko has no other realistic way out. The noose is tightening, and he feels it.

Not that he betrays any concern. I just served him in the wheelhouse, where he's splitting his attention between the ongoing gunfight and a one-sided conversation with none other than the lovely Salome herself. He's romantic, apologetic ... dramatic, certainly. He heaves sighs, he strokes her pitch-black hair. He's always behaved differently around her, you know. I believe he might actually have been in the Marko equivalent of love, up until yesterday when she went too far.

But poor, sad Salome is not responding to Marko's monologue. She stares straight ahead, her marvelous brown eyes unblinking, her pretty face frozen in fear. Which is natural: she's been dead for most of a day. But it makes for awkward conversation.

And now I give you our *plat principal* for the evening: bloody rare roasted leg of garlic-rubbed millionairess—ass to knee, the finest cut—with parsnips and fingerling potatoes, laid on a glittering bed of diamonds and pearls. Voilà!

Fear not the diamonds and pearls; they are every bit as clean as the tray beneath them. And don't they just scintillate? Don't they lend the dish a regal air? But you mustn't eat them, Louis; they're only to gild the frame. I've been saving a bucket of them, and tonight is the night. I've had this idea for ages—'Pearls Before

Swine' I call it—but I could never serve it to my regular guests for fear they'd either choke on the jewels or sneak the greasy things into their pockets. There's nothing millionaires won't try to get away with.

Marko, incidentally, has broken with tradition and requested a non-millionaire main course: braised shank of you, Louis. I gave him another man's leg instead, glazed all over with a hot chipotle gravy to disguise the difference, and served it on a bed of ticking Rolex and Cartier wristwatches. It seemed fitting, given how he's running out of time.

(Salome wants nothing. She's already had her last meal, sad to say.)

I'll tuck in first, shall I? I'm a nervous eater, I must admit, and this is the best thing for nerves. Tender, juicy, bloody red.

The blood of millionaires, as I've said before, is an unparalleled delicacy. It contains the very flavor of their souls, a characteristic essence as identifying as a fingerprint. Millionaires are like snowflakes: no two taste exactly alike. If you concentrate carefully on this meat, Louis, you can intimate a great deal about diet, health, lifestyle. In this blood I detect shopping, drinking, a little cosmetic surgery, mild infidelity, just a hint of antidepressants.

Speaking of blood: you're running a bit low, aren't you Louis? You're pale and slumping. Fear not—the healing power of millionaires will restore you! Just open wide, bite down ... no, don't spit it out Louis! Eat your millionaires, they're good for you. Here, we'll try again ...

Even now, the concentrated essence of that first young man you tasted—his breeding, his good looks, his tan—is integrating itself with your own cells, becoming you, enriching your tissues. Vitamin M, the miracle food. Feel it, Louis. Look alive! Chew!

Amazing as it seems, the magic of millionaires is a natural consequence of their splendid nutritional profile. Millionaires are the best food precisely because they eat the best meals, drink the best wines, enjoy the best lives. They exert themselves in the finest possible ways: horseback riding, orgies, golf. No muscle is unduly strained, no injury goes untreated. In the way they are fed and pampered, millionaires are the Kobe beef of the next century. And that concentration of quality, of all the best things left on this exhausted planet, in perfect balance without the hint of any deficiency, that nutritional excellence and delicate handling produces extraordinary cuts of meat! Just look at the color! See how the juices express when the knife slides in. So tender, so rich with aminos. Such character!

Now I ask you, Louis: is it not my mission, my duty, my calling to deliver the finest and most wholesome foods to the table? Knowing as I do the deep deliciousness of these captains of industry, how can I serve my guests gamey wildebeests, underfed snow leopards, taser-singed bald eagles and all the other exotic crap they bring in? My guests demand the best, they pay for the best, and I, alone among all others, know and am in possession of the best. The very best food there is.

So, yes, discreet substitutions occur. The millionaires are the sauce with which the rest is made palatable. With a few lardons of millionaire to oil the pan, it hardly matters what you braise in it.

There, you have my confession. Were this La Tartine, you could shut me down all over again. But this time you're too late. l'Arche is sinking. My future lies elsewhere.

And that reminds me: I have something I want to show you, that surprise I mentioned. Close your eyes ... Louis? Close your—oh what the hell, leave them open. Anyway here it is:

I've written a book!

All by myself, Louis. Just about fifty thousand words, that pile of paper. It is a treatise on my discoveries, a synthesis of research, experimentation, lore and recipes. A dangerous book, I think. It may not be appreciated in our lifetimes, but on that day when humanity recognizes the vast untapped potential of the millionaire class as its only hope, this book will sell millions. And that day may soon come. Perhaps the revolution brewing in the world's slums will ignite tomorrow. It's not a question of if, only of when.

It's just a first draft, mind you. It may need more work. It might be too long—is it too long? You know how I can ramble and rhapsodize. I've tried to be succinct. But there's so much to say!

The very existence of the millionaires, in the shoddiest of mismanaged countries and at the tops of the most modern western hotels, is an ancient and confounding puzzle. How do they convince the rest of humanity to feed them? How do they dodge the obvious complaint: that they take too much and give too little? In a world of enlightened cooperation they would be banned, taxed, reprimanded, even jailed—or so one would think, but even the socialists have their millionaires. Power simply seems to concentrate, like clots in the blood or lumps in the gravy. In a world of self-interest and greed you'd expect millionaires to be the constant victims of robbery, assault, kidnapping—and true, these things happen, but with nothing near the frequency needed to make a dent in the millionaire problem.

We've seen how they do it, through the invention of overlapping hierarchies of interest—through the bankers, the politicians, the police, the priests, the nervous employees, the paranoid generals. Everyone, it seems, plays his or her part in the fattening of the millionaires. Such a subtle, sophisticated scheme—and it seems to meet so little organized opposition! The desperately poor supermajority of humankind ought to set fire to the millionaires' temples, if only to warm themselves. Instead, they worship the places, dream of moving in someday.

It's brilliant, isn't it? A work of genius, this edifice to the protection, ennoblement and further fattening of the rich. They are so clever, aren't they?

Here's the rub, Louis: they're not. Many of them are smart, somewhat competent, but no match for you or I. An entire second generation of them appear remarkably inept and unsuited to anything. They share a powerful mutual instinct for self-preservation that serves them well, but this glorious structure, this social weave that protects them like a castle on a mountain, this is a building they inherited. The geniuses who designed it are long dead, Louis. The foundation is crumbling, but the millionaires can't see that yet. The millionaires are blind to the coming collapse. They look at everything they have, every advantage tilted toward them, and they tell themselves: I made this, I deserve it, only I could have achieved it, my condition is just and correct. For am I not the mastermind who, armed with tremendous financial and social advantages, managed to go from rich to even richer? And isn't that just the most remarkable, poetic, blessed form of righteousness there is? And how could such a wonderful state of affairs ever end?

Meanwhile: I have read recently that four men of Haiti were imprisoned for digging up and eating their dead relatives. This due to the most recent famine there. It is a thing that happens in famines. Given the few options available, I don't find it particularly gruesome, although I can't imagine it tasted very good.

It is also reported that the slum-dwellers beyond the Parisian périphérique are again rioting, destroying their own homes, shooting their own brothers, raiding their own local grocers for food.

Famine is raging, again, across Africa as a result of the financial disaster. Seeds exist but cannot be planted for financial reasons. Water exists but cannot be used to irrigate; again, finance intervenes. War is brewing again in the Sudan region, where food is so scarce and ammunition so plentiful—both, again, due to the complex interactions between money and humanity.

Tell me, Louis: when are all these poor people going to stop preying upon one another and start preying upon millionaires? If the hungry only knew, only suspected what a heavenly flavor they could be tasting, I'm sure the day would come much sooner.

Ergo: my manuscript! You don't have to read it right this minute, but here it is, for your consideration. It's the only copy; Marko forbids certain records to be kept, so I've had to work secretly, by candlelight, in longhand.

I'm dying to know what you think, Louis. Of course I'm a rank beginner, and this is just a first attempt. I long for your critique, always. Tell me what is most and least effective. I'm sure it's full of cliché and inefficient language, but it's written from my heart. It encapsulates, I believe, my fondest and best wishes for humanity. It's short. Is it too short? How long should such a book be? There's so much I don't know about the book business, Louis. Please teach me.

But you are a busy man and these things take time. First things first. If you're finished with the main course—please, take just one more bite, it will do you good—then let's get you out of this wet little room. As soon as we get moved, I promise, Louis, I will free your hands to turn the pages.

Observe how the Indonesian fishermen managed their catch of mermaids: with these two buttons I open the overhead hatch and lower this hook and chain. Under the arms ... around the back ... I hope this isn't too binding for you.

Louis, please don't thrash around! I know this is hardly a glass elevator but I can't just drag you all up and down the corridors with Marko about, can I? Look on the bright side: once I get you suspended your socks will begin to drip dry.

There. Please be patient with me, Louis. I have to make a very brief appearance topside, and fetch us a new bottle of wine. I trust it will meet your high standards.

Relax, swing gently, and be of good cheer. I'll tuck this manuscript in your coat pocket; it wants to be close to you. Please try not to bleed on it. As I said, it's the only copy.

Up ... up ... up you go! Gently now ... wake up, Louis! You've arrived, finally. Now down, yes, right down here, here's your chair, your blanket. Relax, and let's undo this rigging, and shut this trapdoor before one of us stumbles through it.

Breathe, Louis. Open your eyes, and behold!

Welcome to my bestiary, Louis. Bright, clean and overstocked. All creatures great and small are here sawed and sliced and hung from hooks to be broken down and served up as needed.

If the room below is my slaughterhouse, then this refrigerated storeroom is my surgical theater. It was once a fish freezer; now it maintains a constant three degrees Celsius and a hermetic seal. No rats in here, I'm relieved to say, but you might bump into every other kind of creature.

Look around you. Even forgetting the millionaires, Louis, have you ever seen such variety? Here we have breast of great ape, here is the skin-on flank of a zebra ... the aforementioned giraffe neck, stacked like cordwood, the loin of a mountain lion, the surprisingly tasty tail of the Komodo dragon. Watch it gyrate and sway, left and right, forward and back, dancing with the storm like a chorus line! Be careful, Louis—I wouldn't want you kicked by a dead horse.

All these major cuts, bled and skinned and left to ripen— such a gallery of Nature's art! Animals, stripped of identity, reduced to colors and flavor and lovely structure, assume a beautiful new form. Meat is natural architecture revealed, as by a shipwreck—the sturdy ribbed hulls, the taut lines strung on masts of bone. It's Nature's pattern language employed to solve, in a million unique and clever ways, all the problems of survival: eyes, wings, teeth, tails, undulating spines, multi-chambered hearts ... I am blessed, really, with this opportunity to disassemble living things and see how they tick. I never tire of it.

But butchery is tricky work. It requires a maximum of sympathy, to build trust and limit unnecessary suffering, but a minimum of empathy or one simply can't do it. Its a delicate process that takes great physical strength and steadiness. I don't want to brag but I think I'm particularly suited to it. And I've spared no effort in improving the process for everyone involved.

Lately, Marko and I are called upon to process millionaires as often as twice a week. Our customers are finding it's better to let us do the job, instead of making a mess of things with their guns. It's becoming quite lucrative, too. Having done the hard work of luring a fellow millionaire—an unwanted spouse, uncooperative business partner, stingy kidnap victim or what have you—all the way to Cristobal Minor, onto our boat and down to our special room, our customers will spare no expense to remain innocent of this final messy detail, the punctuation mark on the death sentence.

I think we're worth what we charge. The process we've developed is a delicate, solemn ceremony, calm and liturgical as a Christmas mass. There's candles, a bit of organ music, we wear a special set of spotless white aprons and matching gloves (rubberized nylon for easy cleaning), and of course there is Our Holy Overseer to provide sympathy. We never raise our voices— sometimes I whisper the Shepherd's Psalm for its relaxing effect, while Marko likes to hum Auld Lang Syne—and we are ever cheerful, ever smiling. With our gilded eye and ear protection (against struggle and screaming) we resemble, I hope, something close to angels. In most cases a single blow and a single cut are the worst of it, and the rest is pure ballet. Once stunned and stuck, we hoist them on this same hook-and-chain elevator you just rode, we bleed them, their skin is either singed or stripped, the head comes off, and by the time they're hauled up here they are already mostly transformed from that complicated thing we call "people" to that delicious thing we call "meat". What a mysterious, magical transformation that is.

Here they are, in this corner, a few at least—they have been going fast. Here's a whole carcass, skin off; here is a selection of legs, the meatiest part—although I personally find the arms quite delicious too. (Note the tattoo on this shoulder: "ROOLZ BREAKAH!") The torso doesn't provide much muscle, but the offal is full of delights. I store it all on stainless steel racks, individually wrapped in white paper for quick use. Heads we don't save, for reasons of liability. We toss those over and they sink like stones; at the bottom of the lagoon the eels and crabs make short work of them.

Why don't you take it in, Louis? With so many wonders all around you to behold, why are you staring, so direct and mystified, at plain old me? Such an inquisitive stare, too.

Ah, but I do look a sight, don't I? I appreciate your concern, but don't fret, it's not too severe. I was careful enough to omit the knives, but then, wouldn't you know, he got me with a fork! Over and over, as it happened. But it could have been much worse—an inch to the left and I might have lost an eye.

Speaking of which: I have brought you a small salad of beet-pickled millionaires' eyes on a bed of red sauerkraut, dressed with a dijon vinaigrette and candied hazelnuts. This is a favorite dish of Marko's, although he wasn't having any just now ...

Goddamned Marko. Shovel-faced, sharp-eyed Marko.

He's on to us, Louis. There, I've said it, although it ruins my appetite to do so. He thinks I'm hiding something—the gall of him! He thinks that I, his partner in everything, the one who is the beating heart of this whole operation, the one who brings the millionaires, I who have shared everything—*everything*—I who have never said no as his risky conspiracies deepened, I who introduced him to the pleasures of the table, to real food—and he loves food, our Marko, he loves everything I give him—he now thinks I'm hiding something.

And he knows exactly what it is: it's you. He's a cunning man, but I imagined with all his current troubles that the issue of who, exactly, is coming for dinner would be the furthest thing from his mind. Alas, Marko, genius that he is, is not a rational thinker. He's impulsive, instinctive, perceptive. Like a cat.

He pounces like one too. But fear not: if you can believe it, I've actually had worse. Cuts and bruises, these are the chef's constant companions. Burns, too: see here? This is the third cigarette he's crushed on the same spot.

But, having given him his little outburst, I think we'll be safe from other unreasonable demands in the short term, as long as we take certain precautions.

He's meant to think he's eating you, of course. He specifically asked to eat you; fortunately I still had a fresh millionaire from last weekend, a man of your approximate age and gender, perhaps a bit thicker in the leg, but Marko shouldn't be any the wiser.

Please, don't thank me. I owe you this much. We men of taste must stick together.

The trouble is ... he is the wiser. He suspects us, Louis. He clearly does.

He sniffs his food, you know, very carefully, every bite. He sniffs everything, actually. Our Marko has a rough tongue but a surprisingly acute sense of smell. He has smelled the roast I prepared, marinated in hot spices and fragrant herbs, and through that maze of thick aromas he has navigated to a conclusion.

—What the fuck are you feeding me? is how he put it. As if I'd handed him some rotten egg full of rat poison.

—It's ... the man in question, I replied, trying to sound bored, or nonchalant, or at least relaxed ...

And then he leapt on me with the fork. And, you know, this has happened before. I've learned ... I've learned it will pass. I've certainly learned not to try to escape, not to struggle or fight. It always goes badly when I do that. But he's not so very cruel, he's mostly just *impulsive*. So I lie there on the floor, curled in a ball, protecting the most important parts of me with my hands and arms, and it's all over in a fusillade of stabs and just a few swift kicks. Immediately he sees what he's done to me, his partner, his friend. Immediately I can see the remorse gathering behind his eyes. He's sorry.

—Fuck not with Marko, says Marko. Bring me the head!

—I don't have it, I say! We don't keep heads, you're the one who said the heads are trouble. I know what he's doing: he's trying to save face, to find a polite way out of the impasse, a way he can justify what he's done and salvage his pride. I know he's hurting inside. Whenever he does this to me he's always terribly gentle and sorry later. He's just moody, you know; he's plagued by moods.

The trouble is, Louis—and I'm afraid this is why I'm boring you with this story, in fact—is that Marko was about to let the whole thing drop when something clicked in that amazing mind of his. Marko thought of something, and if it were any other situation I'm sure I'd be purely enthralled by the very cleverness of the man, but as it impacts our current efforts to remain safe and wait out storms I regret to say he's a bit too smart for our own good, our Marko.

Here's the problem: when Marko found you in the kitchen, you struggled. You fought. You did, didn't you? Admit it, there's no shame in it, although of course you shouldn't have. I mean, what I've learned about Marko in these situations is: he always wins. Fighting Marko is like fighting gravity, like arguing with the sea. He's got so much blood in him, such power, and hitting him—or even struggling against him while he's hitting you—

awakens in him a certain fury, a white-hot anger, a blinding delirium of force and cruelty. Fighting with Marko is like fighting hate itself.

And I hardly have to tell you how that went. No, we are both members of another fraternity now: the survivors of Marko.

My question for you is: do you want to stay in our club? Do you want to live, Louis? Please tell me you do. I do. I have, at this point, quite a nuanced relationship with death, and I have lived a long time, longer than some, but air still tastes sweet to me, Louis, the ocean sunrise still stirs poetry in my soul, and yes, I have still so much more important work to do in the area of millionaires. I want to survive this, Louis. Do you?

(While you ponder that, allow me to uncork this darling bottle: 1978 Barolo Monfortino by Conterno, if you can believe it. I found it cowering in a dusty corner; perhaps Salome was saving it for an occasion. To let such a wine sink untasted would be criminal!)

I'm impressed that you're taking your time with my question. Never a glib answer from you, Louis. But allow me to at least assume, for the moment, that you hypothetically want to live. Well, as I said, I believe the best thing we can do is hide out here below, while certain natural forces—Marko chief among them—

interact on the top of the boat. I am still certain this is the right plan. Escape to Cristobal Minor is unlikely even if we were both in a condition to swim. For anything that moves from ship to shore, Marko has a keen eye and a clear shot. Even if he could miss us, the sea wasps are numerous and nasty. Furthermore, now that our relationship with the Cristobos has become so strained, I wouldn't expect much refuge if we reached the shore. Now that they know about Salome, the only things keeping them from swarming the docks and setting us ablaze are the current storm, Marko's well-placed bullets and his terrifying stare.

Escape to the yachts of neighboring millionaires, also, is unlikely. I'm not sure which one you came in with, but they're all unmoored now, anchored far offshore, each a safe distance from the others. I have watched them through the telescope; it seems almost that they're surrounding the island in a coordinated fashion, as if to prevent escape. I saw the arms dealer, Mr. Hazmat, on the deck of his gunboat—he doesn't have the largest yacht, but he does have the largest guns—peering directly back at me through olive drab binoculars. I waved; he did not.

It's a risky position for him, and for all of them beyond the lagoon, because this storm is showing up on our screens and radios as something just shy of a typhoon. But they are millionaires;

they have resources. Most of them, I imagine, will float.

Yes, our best bet is to stay, and hide. Staying is easy; hiding has just become slightly complicated. Marko suspects me. Which would be truly insulting if—well, frankly, even though I am in fact hiding a little secret, even though he's clearly correct in his suspicion, still ... the man ought to trust me! By now, certainly! He ought to be willing to believe his partner, his co-conspirator, his friend. I've never lied to him before, not significantly. It's just one little lie of small consequence to Marko and great personal importance to me, but he has to sniff it out. I'm steamed, I'm boiled, I'm fairly insulted ... although Marko doesn't intend it that way, I know. I understand. It's just ...

Well, at any rate, the trouble is that in your vain but courageous effort of struggling with Marko—earlier, in the kitchen, over that pot of Dinero Escondido—I'm afraid you left a calling card: fingerprints, in blood (yours) on the perfectly white starched buttonholes of a Gucci dress shirt (Marko's). Had today not been so singularly eventful I'm sure that shirt would be safely tumbling in the laundry by now. But today, alas ...

Picture Marko, towering over me. He peers down at his shirt's evidence, sniffs at it ...

—Bring me the mittens, he shouts. By which he means, in

gangster slang, the hands.

—But ... I've got the mittens in brine, I say. Overnight.
They're tomorrow's plait main.

—THE MITTENS! he screams, and then, with his fork—
right here in my cheek! With the ship lurching in the weather,
the wind whipping around in the portholes, Salome's lost eyes
gazing at the scene without focus, and I am cowering, trembling,
on the careening iron wheelhouse floor with Marko's immensity
perched over me like a great human cudgel, as he punctuates
every word with another stab of his fork:

—BRING! ME! THE GODDAMN! MITTENS! AND
SOME GOD! DAMN! KETCHUP!

Then he stops, suddenly remorseful, and returns to his lookout
position at the head table, with his pistol and his knives and his
Salome, and a beautifully roasted leg of barbecued millionaire,
untouched, growing cold.

Sometimes I hate the man. Sometimes I make plans to poison
him. Sometimes I fantasize about doing the deed with my own
hands, but in truth I don't think the element of surprise and the
largest gun I can lift would guarantee the outcome. In truth, I am
afraid.

But also ... you must understand, Marko rescued me. After La Tartine, I had no work. I was unclean, untouchable. No head chef would take a chance on me, no restaurateur would help me rebuild a reputation. Rumors began to spread, legal proceedings began. I fled the continent, but my reputation preceded me, worldwide, in every respectable kitchen. I could not even wash dishes, Louis! I was, in their eyes, nothing more than the man who had been caught red handed.

By you, Louis. Caught red-handed by you.

Now, on the topic of red hands: Marko is up there, right now. Waiting for mittens. And we need to convince him that the meal he's eating is the one he ordered.

Again I ask you, Louis: do you want to live?

If I knew another way, Louis, I'd take it. Don't you think I'd take the other way?

Please sit still. I promise you, I've gotten very good at this. Minimal bloodletting, minimal suffering. You'll want to bite down on this wooden spoon. You're a southpaw, aren't you? So we'll go north. For the purpose of positive identification, one hand ought to do.

Louis! Squirming won't help you, it'll only prolong the problem. If you don't let me apply this tourniquet properly I can't be responsible for the mess.

Please, Louis, do calm down. Breathe.

Perhaps you'd like another sip of wine?

Sip, sip, sip.

Good man. One can lose oneself in a wine this deep. Here, have another swig.

And here's a bit of kitchen wisdom: I've found, Louis, that when I've burned a finger in hot oil, or cut into a thumbnail with the cleaver, or any of the other times that my extremities have misstepped in their daily knife and fire dance, the best trick is to focus elsewhere. On your feet, for instance; are they cold? Or your nose: does it itch? Just think about the rest of you, Louis. Think of the large part of you that will survive this. Your right hand must die so that your other limbs may live—a noble sacrifice for the greater good. The exquisite, sensitive fingers ... they are the body's millionaires, in a way.

Not surprisingly, they are quite delicious. If Marko leaves us any, I'll offer you a taste.

Louis, please speak to me.

Louis, I am prepared to hang on your every word. Do you find me inhuman? Do I deserve Christian hellfire? Just tell me so, and perhaps I will agree. Perhaps I will be swayed by your tremendous eloquence. Tell me what I have forgotten, tell me where I went astray in my pursuit of the greatest good. Or, if I misunderstand that withering stare of yours, by all means please enlighten me. Please Louis ... your words have meant so much to me for so long.

I read your every column in Le Poulet Enchaîné, you know.

Every other month I receive a compilation of past issues from one of our suppliers. It's a scandalous paper at best, meaningless at worst, but until you went on your "unplanned sabbatical" in June I relished your every report on the cuisines of Paris, Berlin, Barcelona, Bangkok, Budapest, Beijing, Seoul, Hanoi ... isolated here as I have been for so long, your words are all I know of my contemporaries.

And Louis: now that it's all over, now that the storm is raging, cleansing the whole island of our experiments, if we survive this night you'll be in a perfect position to deliver your readers a spellbinding story. I see it all in outline: the first rumors, however you encountered them; your disbelief, then your growing suspicion, then your determination (how brave! how true to form!) to investigate personally. Your recruitment of a sympathetic millionaire—I'm still, Louis, deathly curious to know who that may have been—then your penetration of the island, your clever infiltration of the kitchen, and—voilà! The ultimate interview with the ultimate chef!

Such a golden story, Louis, providing only that you live to write it. But I will help you in every way, my friend. Together we will deliver this delicious tale to your hungry audience, and they shall know me, finally, as the explorer, the activist, the pioneer that I am.

Or, conversely, Louis, if you still find me such a monster, well, I won't ask you to sugar the truth. Hew only to your inner compass, Louis. Follow your instincts and your ethics, and damn all the rest. This is the artists's creed, yes? It's mine as well. For we are both artists, Louis, with our own language and our own visions.

But Louis, please: won't you speak? Even during the surgery, when I confess I might have hoped to hear your lovely voice cry out in pain, you remained silent as a fish, quiet as a lamb. Your eyes, Louis, great big and bloodshot as they are, speak volumes. They betray your intelligence, your cunning and quickness. But I long, Louis, to feel the carefully creased edges of your well-chosen words, delivered in your quiet, intelligent voice.

I know you're not feeling well—*obviously!*—and I am sorry. It's been a hard day for everybody. But we're winning, Louis. I know that down here all you can perceive is the ship tossing us like salad, and the rhythmic tenderizing of the hull by the piers. You are like the blind man who rides on top of the elephant— and you don't even get to use your hands. So let me paint you a picture.

The report from topside is interesting, complex. First of all, your sacrifice was not in vain: Marko seems satisfied. I brought him the requested appendage, on ice, lightly salted. I had a suitable explanation prepared for the lack of a matching mitten, but he didn't even ask.

On the shore, the group of Cristobos clustered behind the guardhouse has grown to several dozen, and others have taken up positions behind every noteworthy large object. They're stirred up like ants, all of them—also plastered with rain and tilted sideways by wind, but they hardly seem to notice the weather. They're far too poor for guns, but they may be planning some kind of banzai charge with epithets and fishhooks. As I arrived, Marko had just shot one man creeping towards us on the underside of the dock; I think it might have been Raoul, one of our waiters. I watched Marco pump a few more bullets into the thoroughly dead young man, and then a swarm of crabs clambered up onto the pier and started picking him apart.

In the water, chaos reigns. The few ships that have stayed moored, including our own, seem to be bashing the timbers of the authentically rickety dock into splintery flotsam. One small yacht in the harbor has actually capsized, and a millionaire and two underlings are cowering in an inflatable dinghy, fearing for their lives I'm sure. Marko drew an exploratory bead on them with his longest gun, but he hasn't fired yet—a wise course of inaction, I think. Firearms are the great equalizer; they counteract all of his natural advantages.

Then Marko returned to his seat, still eyeing the docks through the window like a watchful toad, still stroking the hair of the dead Salome. I brought him the mitten, as I described, and he fixed me with a questioning gaze: childlike, searching, disarming actually. I had to will myself mightily to believe in our ruse, while lying as little as possible.

—Here is the ingredient, I said, the knuckles you asked for. It's uncooked, and to do it justice will take ...

He didn't listen. There in the silver ice bucket it glistened, briny and wet, stiff and blueish, only slightly unclenched from the tight fist you held it in. It could have been mistaken at a distance for an octopus, or a nervous starfish, or perhaps a crown of white sausage. It existed in that curious limbo you see all around you in this cooler: it used to be a man, it wasn't yet a meal. One could vividly imagine either end of its history, or both at once.

It's exactly that shock, you know, that dissonance of a pig's intelligent eyes superimposed upon a plate of pork chops, that drives certain souls into the vegan camp. I tell you, Louis, if vegetables had faces ...

But I digress. What Marko did with your hand was very curious. First he impaled it on a steak knife and lifted it daintily over his plate. As brutal as he is wont to be, he is a delicate diner, fastidious with knife and fork. Then, holding it to his face, he closed his eyes and sniffed deeply from each fingertip, ran his snout along the back of the hand, buried it in the crook between index finger and thumb, placed the palm over his nose as if covering his own face ... snorting, huffing, sniffing like a bloodhound all the while. And the smell—the smell of you—it seemed to intoxicate him somehow. I do believe I heard a single sob hitch in his great chest, and then he clutched your hand to his breast, and sighed.

I was already slowly backing away from this scene when a remarkable thing happened. You may have heard it down here: one of the great windowpanes of tempered glass in the wheelhouse exploded inward, admitting the full fury of the storm, and Marko dropped down to the floor, clutching a suddenly bloody ear!

Some sniper had taken his shot. I can't be sure if the bullet came from shore or from a distant yacht, but Marko seemed to have some idea. I slunk out of the cabin on my belly, with your discarded hand in mine, as he took up a gunnery stance in a shielded corner of the empty window frame.

In my retreat I heard him fire two rounds, and nothing in

return. Knowing Marko, I imagine he found his mark.

You see? These are the forces, this is their dance. With one stroke, Marko has alienated the entire field of millionaires. When the storm passes they will tighten the noose. There's a dozen agile, well-armed ships nearby, I don't think even Marko can shark his way out of this one.

He may have some plan. That dull diesel roar of our generators, I'm sure you've noticed, has been complimented by a much louder rumble and a certain rattling: these are the main engines of l'Arche, it pains me to realize, come to life for the first time in ages. I cannot tell you when they've last been oiled, or maintained in any way, and they do seem to sputter and skip. I wouldn't put much faith in them, but perhaps Marko is formulating a final bluff.

I'll mourn him when he's dead, Louis. A friend, a mentor, a savior, a unique and complex man. A man who taught me what I'm capable of. The world will be smaller without him.

But you and I, Louis, if we are quick and careful, we will survive. I have an excellent alibi prepared; better yet, I have a boat. It waits for us on the opposite edge of the island: a small two-sheeter, up on blocks but easily launched, on which we might sail to the mainland.

And from there? Then, Louis, the game begins anew!

I am already setting the tables, in my mind, of the next great restaurant. Our restaurant, Louis. You've always shied away from partnerships in them, I know. But now that you've tasted the meat of the gods, now that you know what millionaires can do, I know you're with me, Louis. With your connections, and the not insignificant bundles of dollars and euros and yuan I've stashed away in these last lucrative months, we can make a fresh start. The market wants us to succeed, Louis—l'Arche has awakened a powerful demand. There are still, more and more, hungry insolent needy millionaires queueing up, demanding to be fed, demanding to be eaten.

I know a perfect location on the outskirts of Ciudad Juarez— on land, Louis, blessed land! I tell you, this whole era of l'Arche has sometimes felt like a banishment at sea. I've mastered the art of chopping on a slanted table, steadying pans on burners that rock and pitch, but the things we could do on land, Louis, are far beyond what's possible here. With a staff of six we could serve fifty tables on a dozen millionaires a night!

Things are looking up, Louis! My plan is working, the tides are turning both literally and figuratively. Cheer up! It depresses me to see you so glum. After all, your own great sacrifice has made the crucial difference.

Speaking of which: I have a treat for you.

Now, given your Sphinxish silence, one might still admit some doubt on your stance, overall, regarding the millionaires. Certainly you haven't condemned me. You haven't called me names, demanded my execution, told me to stop. I can't help but be encouraged, Louis; I have to assume some consent in your silence. I thought I saw the hint of pleasure in your eye when you tasted the boudin noir, but that is nothing compared to what I am about to offer you.

However, if you have qualms ... say, you fear for your soul in some post-mortem courtroom, or you are concerned, perhaps, about the poor poor millionaires—not that they are concerned about you, Louis—or, more likely, supposing that the unfortunate, unusual, unruly circumstances surrounding your first meal at l'Arche have left you wishing to postpone major ethical decisions ... well, I can't blame you for that. I know where your heart will lead you. I'm your friend, Louis. I'm not about to pressure you to eat millionaires, people you don't even know.

But answer me this, Louis: what would be the objection, what could be wrong, evil, unseemly or ethically problematic about eating *yourself*? Are you not the master of your own domain? Is it not the right of all creatures to own and use their bodies how they see fit for their own survival, health and happiness?

Louis, I now present you: Fist of De Gustibus à la Pommes Frites! This my favorite way to enjoy a fresh hand. I've split the knuckles to make bite-sized pieces, beer-battered and flash-fried them—believe me, approaching the deep fryer in this bobbing and pitching context is no mean feat—then mounded them atop a white wine and shallot gravy thickened with blood—fear not, it's only yours—and a pinch of millionaire fat, which you may avoid, if you truly object, by dipping it in this house-made ketchup instead. A sprinkling of pulled panda meat, and a side dish for the bones ... there you have it! It's a twist on the poutine craze that you wrote about in February.

You see, Marko had completely lost interest in your hand, and you know I abhor waste. I thought, well, Louis De Gustibus is no millionaire—that is, I imagine you live on a simple journalist's salary, sufficient for a life of the mind. You go to plays, visit the opera, subscribe to many journals, own many books, but economize in other areas ... that is the writer's life, is it not?

And yet, Louis, you *eat* like a millionaire. In fact, if anyone is more likely to have drank finer wines, dined on finer cuts, ingested a wider variety of nature's best beasts than the millionaires who circulate through both ends of this vessel, it's a highly esteemed and influential food critic such as yourself.

Consider what gives millionaires their dazzling properties. I believe it is partly that their composition is almost exactly the same as our own. Any other food, the teeth must first grind it to paste, the stomach then has to boil it in acids to break it down further, down to the simplest amines and scraps of protein, and then out of that molecular wreckage the body must painstakingly stitch together the distinctly human cells and hormones and juices and bones. But millionaires offer plug-and-play nutrition; all the microscopic building blocks of human tissue arrive properly sized, stacked and numbered. To the human gut it's the difference between a seven course restaurant meal and chewing on a raw dead rodent, bones and all

So consider then, Louis, what your digestion will do when you introduce a piece of the very same body in which it operates? Why, it will be like an immigration officer meeting his own mother at the border, arms outstretched. Rejoice, says the meat: I have returned! Darling, says the stomach: we have missed you so! I can't imagine anything more fortifying to the health, more agreeable to the constitution. It's just what you need right now, Louis: you are not looking well at all.

Listen, Louis: I'm going to free your hands. That is, your remaining hand, your good left hand. I think it's time. Soon we may need action from it. Meanwhile, this poutine is finger food, it's hot and wants to be eaten right away. And I think we've gotten beyond the baby bird business, haven't we? If your continued bondage is the grudge you're holding, then be free. I only ask that you keep your right arm elevated, because your tourniquet is dripping just a bit and I'd hate for you to pass out. So please, enjoy the aroma while I make a few more cuts with the waiter's friend.

Smell that, Louis. That fragrance, so unique and primal. Have you ever wondered what your body does with those particles of aroma that enter through the nose? Are they exhaled, or do they enter the bloodstream? Is it possible that everything we smell, we have in a microscopic way already begun to eat?

There's a story about a beggar who flavors his one small scrap of bread by holding it over the delicious steam rising from a shawarma vendor's rotating stack of roast lamb. The vendor, seeing how his odors are being hijacked by this destitute figure, demands payment for the service. The beggar agrees: he tells the vendor, for the odor of your meat, I will pay you with the smell of my money.

Aha! There you are, Louis. Your good left hand, free at last. Stretch out your arms and let them circulate. Your feet are still tied, but we'll cope with that in due time. Hot food doesn't wait!

I'm sorry I didn't untie you sooner, but you know, trust is a fragile thing. Really, I should have trusted you sooner. Time has flown. I do trust you, Louis, completely. And I am thankful, so very thankful for the opportunity, finally, to explain myself. Perhaps I talk too much, but I thank you, Louis, for listening. Now please, dig in!

And ... I would never presume such a thing, of course, but with your permission, and only if you're completely comfortable with the idea ... I know: I promised I wouldn't eat you. But Louis old man, you do smell wonderful! Your hand, I mean. Just that, that alone.

So ... would it offend you ... do you mind if I have a taste? I know I've eaten the lion's share tonight, I don't normally have such an appetite, but this is not a standard night at all.

Any objections? Please, just say the word if you are the least bit put off. I would understand completely. I am your friend, Louis.

Yes? No?

Very well. But after you, Louis. You are the guest, I am the host.

Ah, yes! Louis, you have finally come around! Isn't it rich? Isn't it succulent? And finally, Louis, I see your radiant smile! I shouldn't hover over your enjoyment, but I do love to feed a hungry man. Flavor doesn't lie, does it? No, your poor body is calling out for food, Louis, and food has come to rescue you ...

Louis! Wake up! Don't fade on me now. You've fainted right in your poutine. Please, stay with me. You've had enough wine, I think, but can I get you some coffee? Hot coffee, yes, that's the thing—and then action!

As soon as those men on the dock make their move, we will make ours. There's a covered lifeboat, a dinghy for two on the port side. As soon as Marko gives us some maneuvering room we'll quietly lower ourselves off this doomed boat. We can row out of harm's way and transfer to my escape vessel, stocked with sausages and jerky aplenty for sailing to the coast. Everything we need, Louis, for the next step.

Oh dear, I haven't heard that chain rattle in ages. Is he weighing the anchor? I'd better look into this. You stay here, stay quiet. Go ahead and finish the fries without me, I'll be right back. If Marko comes in, just play dead. I dare say you'll do that well—you look like meat already.

Look alive, Louis! I bring hot coffee, fine cheese and fresh news. The storm is lifting and our restaurant, unfortunately, has set sail, limping away from a swarm of furious torch-wielding Cristobos on their mutilated dock.

Our captain has entered a manic swing. He's been on the radio to a few of the neighborhood millionaires, attempting to organize some kind of assistance, call in a few favors. But they won't be coming. Their yachts are all around us, maintaining a thousand meter radius, guns turned toward us like a herd of aristocratic hunters on horseback preparing to execute a fox.

Marko is undaunted. He paces in the wheelhouse, smoking cigarettes and cooing to Salome, suffering spasms of laughter as blood drips from his ear.

The rich are going to win this round, as usual. What has Marko got to meet them with? True, we do have one significant cannon under a tarp on the bow—Mr. Hazmat is a remarkable salesman—but the one time Marko ever fired the damn thing we nearly capsized. The threat of the cannon might keep the millionaires at bay a little while; they do hate to scratch their lovely ships. But they only need to hold us here and wait for us to sink. In fact, they've won already. They've timidly pressed their enormous advantages. That's all it takes when you're rich.

It's just not fair.

You know why the revolution never comes, Louis? It's because people are good. People are basically good. People hate conflict, cruelty, fighting in general. I don't mean the millionaires—they are the exception to every rule, aren't they?—but just about everybody else on earth naturally resists the temptation to go to war, to kill their neighbors, to savor vengeance. Our cleverest politicians must work hard and harness vast resources in order to inspire warlike feelings in their citizenry, to generate the hatred and fear needed to raise armies. It doesn't come easily or naturally to decent people.

And those revolutionaries, who appeal always to the best in us—to our sense of justice and fairness and our love of peace and plenty, to international brotherhood and an end to prejudice— their very goodness undermines any sinister momentum they can generate toward a siege upon the ruling classes.

And so the millionaires always win. Always.

That's why my book is so very necessary. Because I have outlined, right here in these pages, a completely new system of thought—well, actually an ancient and forgotten one, newly contextualized. In summary, I propose that we embrace the rich as a sacred class—as we already do, you see—and that, like virgins to the volcanos or prisoners upon the Aztec altars, we undertake this miraculous millionaire diet, not out of hatred or envy, but rather out of love, admiration, caring. Let us husband them well, the millionaires. Give them their yachts, their many homes, many cars, many hand-stitched suits of clothing. Send them to the best schools and largest boardrooms. This is what makes them millionaires—what makes them fat and rich and wholesome. Give them the best life that an edible creature could possibly live. It's what the new organic cattle ranchers have tried to do with their beef, of course, but to a far greater degree than has ever been attempted—indeed to the greatest degree possible! Spare no effort in fattening the rich, work for them and tithe to them and massage them and groom them and put their needs always ahead of our own. As it has always been, so let it remain.

Until! Until that day comes when we require their *sacrifice*, for the greater good. Oh, the ceremony of it: picture this year's wealthiest industrialists proceeding to the regal altar, bedecked in finest Gucci and Versace, encrusted all over with fourteen karat gold jewelry and sophisticated personal electronics. We shall thank them publicly, cheer them sincerely, stun them carefully, slaughter them with dignity and roast them with joy. Let every member of the community receive their portion, a communion in the faith of markets and money. Let us restore balance to capitalism. Us—you and me, Louis!

I see a thought, Louis, stalking in that room behind your eyes. You are thinking: the millionaires will be slow to embrace this plan. Rare and lovely is the pig that asks to be eaten. But in this proposed scheme—in the book I call it Ethical Carnivisim, but I'm not sure that's the best phrase, I crave your advice on this among many other questions—but in my proposed scheme there is even an incentive for the millionaires.

You've observed their competitiveness, their love of the extraordinary, their desire to convince themselves they belong on a higher plane. And you've probably noticed, as I have here in the environs of l'Arche as well as in other rooms, other restaurants, that the modern multiplication of millionaires does not please the millionaires themselves. No, not at all. They don't wish their ranks to swell, it makes them feel less special.

So imagine if, in every community, the millionaires themselves are granted the responsibility of choosing the honorable victim, the fatted calf? How would they go about it, do you think? Oh, the clever millionaires, they would propose methods of chance, of justice, of cunning—contests, trials, subterfuge, market solutions perhaps. What a great, grand game it will make for them. I dare say, Louis, they will thrive on it.

And then at the close of their selection, when one millionaire is cast from the fold, well, won't the rest of them feel that much more elite, that much more successful and deserving? I tell you, Louis, they will need powerful convincing at first, but one day the millionaires will insist the entire idea was their own.

That's just a summary of my plan, Louis. This manuscript contains all the details, all the explanations, the frameworks, the justifications, and of course there's a set of favorite recipes and handy techniques for making the most of this fantastic new resource. Once people taste what they're missing there will be a positive frenzy for it.

It goes far beyond nutrition, you know. Millionaires are like pigs: every part is useful! Look at my hair, Louis. I am not a vain man but I believe it's a matter of record that this hair of mine is thick, lustrous, smooth. It's the hair of my youth, Louis, but not long ago it was a fraying, clumping mess, alarmingly thin on top. The sea wind used to sting my pate and the sun used to burn it. No longer! And the miracle salve that restored my youth is none other than the rendered fat of millionaires, blended with just a smidgen of pâté de testicule. It keeps my skin supple, it accelerates the healing of cuts and bruises, and I find the aroma intoxicating—don't you?

There is so much yet to explore with this material. The skins, the bones, the hair, the teeth, it's all such fabulous first-class stuff. Every single part of a millionaire is impregnated with the essence of wealth. Science needs to study the supernatural effects of this food. It is like eating angels plucked from clouds.

What do you say, Louis? Will you help me change the world? Will you help me harvest the angels' power? Will you help me feed the masses?

Louis, speak to me. Why won't you speak?

Oh Louis, you're not well at all. Have you pissed yourself? You have, oh my. And your big ears, they're drooping like wilted cabbage. Your lips have grown blueish and your little visible puffs of breath are coming smaller and less frequently. I even notice, if you don't mind my saying so, a bit of drool creeping from the corner of your mouth.

You're positively dying, Louis! I do not understand it, but you are. Why? What did Marko do to you? You've suffered some blows, of course, but I've seen men your age take much worse abuse and keep on struggling, sometimes for days.

Please hang on, Louis. Sip some coffee, warm yourself, fortify yourself. I know the news is discouraging, but escape is still possible, even likely. It's a matter of patience and attention—our moment will come! We must be ready to seize it. Once we're in the lifeboat, I can rush you to a fine modern hospital in a matter of days, a week at the latest ...

This is more than just a thrashing from Marko, isn't it? There's something else wrong with you. You appear, Louis, to be suffering from a pre-existing condition. If I can be candid: even when you first arrived you looked like hell.

Is ... Is that why you won't speak to me? My God ... can you not speak at all? You can't can you? Some paralysis of the tongue? A stroke, a tumor, a spinal injury? What was it, Louis? Oh, but you'll never tell me ...

You cannot speak! Louis De Gustibus, the lifelong journalist and lecturer, has lost his voice! Oh, my poor friend! Oh Louis ... this is why your articles have disappeared! This is the cause of your hiatus, I see it now.

What a cad I've been, how insensitive, asking you all this time to speak. When I'm sure nothing would bring you greater pleasure ... oh, please forgive me, Louis! I was only ignorant, and proud.

But what's the cause? A blow to the head? A stroke? Did a blood vessel burst in the hardest working part of your brain to knock out just the crucial portion, just the golden center of your mind? Or an autoimmune disease? Mad cow? A dementia in your family genes? But what of these other symptoms ... is it cancer? Cancer everywhere? Raging through the body? Yes? I read your tearful eyes, Louis. But is there truly no cure, nothing doctors can do to slow the progress? Nothing you'd be willing to endure? I've heard the cures of cancer can be worse than the disease ... oh Louis, you're dying! You were dying when you got here!

I get it now, Louis: you *came here to die!* You came here with a last wish, one only I could fulfill—oh Louis! Dear friend! I'm moved to tears! Oh, if this only could have been a better day. If you had come even yesterday we could have had it all—the dining room, the fine art and candlelight, the many plates, the gentle rolling of a calm sea. I would have done all I could to make your last meal the very finest of your life. And this sad substitute—hiding, bleeding, freezing, tied up in twine, fretting over the moods of that mad beast upstairs—Louis, you deserved so much better. I have failed you.

But I will not desert you. Stay with me, Louis, just a little bit longer and we will beat him, together. Revenge will be our entremets, freedom our digestif.

Louis, we've known each other a long, long time. We know each other well. And I know how much you love me. The ethics, the ... problems ... I haven't been easy to love. But if you close your eyes to all of the things I've done, good or bad, and concentrate on the flavors, the aromas, the sensations that I have given you ... I know I am your favorite. I know that I am the favorite chef of the world's greatest gourmet! I forgive you for everything you ever wrote about La Tartine, for the things you never wrote about l'Aubergine, none of that matters now. You did what you felt was right. And you have returned to me, Louis! Where once I doubted, now I am sure.

Love's a tricky thing for me, Louis. As you know, there are certain joys of nature that I am simply not allowed. Women, in particular: I mustn't. You told me I mustn't, and you were right, and honestly Louis you should be proud of how I've mastered this hunger of mine. But love is more than eros, it is philos and agape, adoration, appreciation, familiarity ... I love Marko, you know; in many ways we are almost married. We complete each other, Marko and I. Together we have done things we never could alone.

But you, Louis, are the one whose attention I always craved. You are the one to whom I made love, all those many nights at the old bistro, fixing your favorites—I actually redesigned our menu, you know, based around what I could find of your preferences in the microfiche. Did you realize, Louis, how deeply I studied you, how meticulously I watched you? How I seduced you, Louis? How I ground my teeth with anxiety as I peered through the service window to watch you eat that first meal? You wielded your silverware with such gravity, such surgical intent, such destructive potential! I struggled to interpret your every motion, but you left no clues. Wordlessly, inscrutably you laid down your spoon, made marks in your little book, paid, donned your coat and exited into the rain. I slept not a wink that night, I was a useless bag of nerves and questions. But how I trembled with excitement when you returned the very next day! Oh, how I fussed and slaved over every dish you ordered. Did you imagine you hadn't been spotted? Did you think I hadn't already visited the library to find your photo in the archives? I even followed you, Louis, when you left l'Aubergine. I followed you to the Café Grincheux where you took tea, and from there all the way to your apartment, and I watched your window until the light went out that night, all the time wondering, hoping, searching for a sign.

The other diners? They meant nothing, they were props, decoration, part of my elaborate ruse to convince you that you were not the apple of my eye. I didn't want to scare you, Louis. Like a delicate, nervous bird you alighted on my doorstep and I wanted only to feed you, to examine your beauty and stoke the flame of life inside you.

Of course I began to expect, at some point, that a positive review was forthcoming. After all, a gourmet does not eat ten times in the same restaurant because he hates the food! And I knew, Louis, the shattering effect of your positive press. L'Aubergine was deep in debt, my backers were demanding schedules and improvements; they were on the verge of meddling in the most destructive ways. I worked harder, I held my ground, the tension became extreme and I'm afraid, as you know, my bad habits began to assert themselves.

But one good review from you, Louis, would have transformed that tension from the desperate cling of survival to the grinding pace of instant success. One good review from Louis De Gustibus guarantees at least six months of overbooked dining rooms filled with fickle, demanding aesthetes. The Avalanche, that is what we call a positive De Gustibus review in the kitchen: long hours, intense pressure, a kind of madness. It would have been a good problem to have, don't get me wrong. It would have pleased my backers, made my reputation and allowed me, eventually, to escape.

Knowing the Avalanche was coming, I appreciated your humility that much more. You, alone in the dining room with the one waiter, savoring each sip of wine as you made little marks in your moleskine. I kept my distance until you asked to meet me. Do you remember the first lovely conversation we had? With such brilliance you critiqued the profiteroles! How I adored your clarinet voice, the clipped precision of your syllables. Was I too nervous and clumsy? Did I trip over my words? It had been such a confusing, hopeful, desperate time.

And I don't blame you for what happened. I blame myself, of course. I blame my hunger. My problem.

My problem is simple: I eat people. I can't not. I've had this problem for a long, long time. I crave it, Louis, I crave the flavor. Food without men in it has ceased to have any taste or meaning to me. Like an addict I have quit and un-quit, broken so many vows that quitting again would be a tasteless joke. And I have questioned my creator who gave me this craving, and consulted all the philosophers, and wondered long and hard: am I simply evil? Do good and evil exist? Is killing always wrong? Could I eat only the bodies of condemned criminals, for instance, and if I could, would I then cease to be, as you once called me, a monster? Is the problem my unique and difficult appetites, or is it my failure to control them? All my life, Louis, I have juggled and struggled and pondered and wept, yes, wept for my victims, for though they were delicious they were also alive and beautiful once.

But I have always noticed, always known, that all my comrades in the human species share an idiotic blindness toward their own cruel consumption of birds, beasts and fish—beautiful electric living creatures all. To me, it borders on the sociopathic. They do not think about what happens in the murder factories, they do not take up the question of right and wrong in butchery. They hold their noses and shovel forkfuls of torture, disease and hormones into themselves. They know just what they're eating; they simply don't care.

I care very much, Louis. All my life I've aimed to strike a balance, a comfortable and defensible ethical stance. I've gone without as long as I could, and when I fed soup to the needy I fortified it with the flesh of only the most hopeless, dissolute alcoholics, gutter-bound failures soon to die in one way or another. And when I fed you that roast of lamb at l'Aubergine? Trust me, that little girl never felt any pain. It all happened in a flash as she was sleeping.

Your review never came, Louis. And you never returned again, after that meal. A meal you finished with gusto, I recall. L'Aubergine withered on the stalk, the financiers shut me out, and I set fire to the place and fled Paris entirely, certain that you knew, certain that my time was up.

Did you know, Louis? I've often wondered if you recognized the flavor of that little girl from some previous misadventure of your own. But you neither praised or panned my bistro, and the police never took an interest, desperate as they were for clues all year. You let me down, Louis, but perhaps you also saved me.

And I will save you in return, Louis. Do not give up! Our moment of advantage will come—soon!—and we will seize it with three hands. In preparation, let me replace my beloved manuscript in its waterproof diver's pouch and hang it around your neck like so. Please try not to be shot while wearing this, Louis! You are the life preserver, the flotation device. You must rescue what I have wrought, my precious contribution, my child. We will make it off this boat, and I will deposit you in a hospital on the mainland, with my masterpiece to keep you company, and then I'll slink away and vanish. I have tried my best to create good things with the ingredients I was given. Now it's time for the world to taste, and to criticize.

I know you'll treat me fairly, Louis. I read your mind. Only you see me as the thing I am, the animal and the man. You never judged me, Louis. Lord knows I've judged myself, failed myself.

I once thought I was so evil, I tried to drown myself in the Seine. Then later I believed the opposite, that I was a kind of angel tuned to play a mysterious, noble part. But really I am none of these things. I am simply a repository, Louis, for a hunger far greater than myself. A man cannot be noble on an empty stomach, Louis, and my own constitution requires taboo flesh. It's not my requirement, Louis, it's the hunger. It too is an elemental force.

Do you like the cheese? Try the cheese. Enjoy the cheese, it is fine stuff. It's Urda, from Transylvania. The favorite cheese of Vlad the Impaler. Oh, how we dote upon the world of fine cheeses, all the various splendid types, each concentrated from mother's milk, each ripened with centuries of evolved skill. Such majesty!

But Louis: I hate the goddamned cheese! I cannot stand the delicately caramelized brussels sprouts. Potatoes Dauphinoise disgust me. Rotisserie quail stuffed with their own eggs appall me. Beef Bourgenoise bores me, honey-roasted ham depresses me, and sirloin steak is as empty as tofu. These animals of the earth, these exotics dangling all around us, are each and every one imbued with characteristic and curious flavor—honestly, I really do recommend the mountain lion, for you or anyone else—but for me, Louis, there is only one food, only one thing. There only ever has been. I can prepare all the rest to perfection, infuse it with high style and a certain culinary sarcasm that my guests mistake as ultimate sincerity. But I am a cannibal, an eater of men. It's a specific, constant craving that resonates in my skeleton—the smell of human meat rings me like a bell. It was never a choice for me, like it is for the millionaires; it is how I was made, and I cannot apologize.

Cannibals have always existed, Louis, and we always will. In nature, cannibalism is as regular as famine. Pigs, fish, worms and people: when pushed to starvation's edge, they will take steps. It's the oldest story, garbled as it may be.

Picture, if you can, the first woman. Some calamity has forced her entire gangly, hairless herbivore clan down out of their family tree and across the wide African plains on freshly evolved legs tuned for endurance. For days and for weeks she runs, in light and in darkness, on land and through water, separated from her tribe, pursued by who know what prehistoric predators, until one day she crosses over to a new world, and finds herself alone in a landscape unlike any her race has ever known. Until this day, she has only ever gathered and sprinted, eaten and ran, subsiding on the tough and infrequent morsels of the dry savanna, but now ... now she has stumbled across a garden, one of unparalleled beauty and sustenance.

Call her Eve. She has the seed-crushing molars of a herbivore, a sensitive tongue for sorting out tiny inedibilities, and while she's perhaps enjoyed a crispy locust or a paste of termite grubs upon her meals of dusty roots and bitter leaves, she's not what you and I would call a gourmet, not yet. Hunger has always been her constant companion, food her absent friend. But today, she is the first human to discover fruit—individually-wrapped snack packs of sugar and vitamins, positioned at eye level, dangling all around her. Bananas and plantains, perhaps, or pomegranates, or apples, almost certainly apples. A few well-adapted megafauna might reach the higher fruit first, but here, in this garden, nature has provided plenty for all.

An end to hunger! Is that where mankind's story begins? On that first day that everyone was fed and sheltered and needed only to digest and be happy, and to think? Our Eve, she must think it's a dream. Truly, if miracles can occur, this was the first.

She would stay, of course, as long as she could. She would climb every tree, taste everything the animals tasted and other things besides, master this new landscape and dream of the day when others would arrive to share it.

Poor young Eve. There is so little she knows about the world. What would she make of the growing lump in her belly, this presence that seems to push and poke from inside? Why, she must have been knocked up back in Africa, by a cousin or brother perhaps, before the tribe was scattered. But what does lonely Eve know of this? She ran, she found this place, she ate the fruit and now something has taken root inside her.

Eve is strong, close to nature. Alone behind some shrub she bravely bears her child, and he lives. Let's call him Adam, shall we? Now there are two, one sprung from the ribs of the other. Eve looks at this second little miracle, all hungry and pleading. It's made of me, she realizes. People are made of people! And perhaps she tries to share her apples, her grapefruit, oranges, lemons, but the little offspring only wants one thing. Eve is a clever girl, though unschooled; she figures it out. Soon the baby is sleeping fitfully, and Eve ponders this new mystery, this latest strangeness: he's eating me. The baby eats the mother, drinks her like a bottle.

And now Hunger, that old passenger briefly forgotten, returns to visit. Adam is ravenous, Eve is famished. She eats for two—perhaps she begins to see the limits of her windfall. Perhaps she eats the very last apple of the season, and then the temperate weather shifts, and the storms come, and the ripe things fall and rot, and fortunes change.

She looks up the trees, climbs to the top of them with crying Adam on her back, seeking a sign, another miracle. Rain comes, and icy wind. Leaves turn black and cover the ground with slime. This is her first winter; she is the first human ever to winter this far north. Creation is a fickle friend, now giving, now taking. And as much as she searches all outdoors for assistance, the only voice she hears comes from inside herself: old familiar Hunger, curling through her belly, simmering and squeezing and nipping at her heart. Hunger is the insistent stomach, the needy intestines, the serpent coiled within, the reptile that came before the mammal grew up around it. From the reptile mind at the base of the brain, hunger whispers to Eve. She's cold, she's hungry, the baby is crying and there is nothing, nothing at all, left to eat.

Nor is Eve the only hungry one. At night there are footsteps below the sleeping tree. Hungry roaming animals, one by one, wander through the fallow garden—just as cold, just as desperate, just as deserted by Nature, but armed with sharp canines and claws. They smell her, Louis. They don't know what she is, but she smells delicious. And they, too, have snakes inside of them, gnawing and demanding.

While little Adam cries, and cries, and cries.

Eve says: just yesterday I had everything, and now it's all gone. What will I do? Where will I go? Shall I run again, run until the beasts of the night take me down and eat me, eat my child?

Excuse me, says the serpent, I couldn't help overhearing. What was that last bit? Those last three words you said?

Shut up snake! says Eve. I have nothing for you. There's no food here. Nothing left to eat.

And the serpent says: Oh, but there is still one thing. Something that's made out of you. Something that was in your belly once, and could be again. Something that's never had qualms about nibbling at *you*. Something that makes an awful racket, day and night. Something that, given your current fortunes, you might do better without.

You can always make another one, the serpent says. And doesn't he smell sweet, like ripe strawberries? Isn't he so soft and tender you could just chew him to pieces? So hard to keep alive, so easy to kill.

Eat the baby, Eve. Put him back in your belly and wait for springtime.

And it's just not fair: ten thousand years later, this ancient story is garbled in every way but the one thing that never shifts is the blame. Eve should never have listened to that snake, they say. She should have just said no. She should have prayed for a miracle. And that is our official policy on hunger, worldwide, to this day. Yes, it's regrettable that starvation makes you insanely desperate, but for God's sake don't get all worked up about it, don't do anything rash—like looting the grocer, or burglarizing the banks, or preparing free meals for the destitute and homeless without first obtaining a health permit and a parade permit and a variance. Instead, it might help to pray to God for forgiveness; he's clearly pissed off at you. But it's nothing to do with us, insist the global fat and the global smug. It's a matter of history, sin, market forces, those sorts of things. Please return to your favelas and quit eating your babies.

Eve survived that winter, and had other babies, but her reputation was done for. Every other bipedal hairless hominid who eventually caught up with her in that agricultural wonderland was quick to judge, on a full stomach, the thing she did on an empty one. So she left, and others arrived, and they too were ambushed by the sudden onset of this new thing called winter, and they too were both corrupted and saved by that useful forbidden knowledge:

When times are tough, people are made of people.

And speaking of tasty people ... don't take this the wrong way, Louis, but I just have to mention that I am fairly stunned by how fragrantly delicious you are! Tell me, having tried the pommes frites yourself, comparing them to the boudin noir, don't you find this one clearly superior? But you haven't quite the experience of this stuff on the palette that I have, so let me assure you: you really do taste like the very best millionaires, Louis. Perhaps even better! Of course you are by vocation well-fed, but still, there are unique, exquisite notes in your flavor, a hint of soft, nutty bitterness in the juices that's entirely new to me. It's quite remarkable. It makes me wonder what you've been eating lately.

Don't worry, your survival is both urgent and imminent, I guarantee that. But if you weren't such a dear friend, if I didn't need you so badly to help me bring my message to the world, well, I have to admit that upon your entirely consensual, humane and regrettable death I would be hard pressed not to taste just a little bit more. It's a sin to waste food, you know.

But put all that out of your mind. Hang on, Louis, our time is coming. I can tell we're out at sea—the engines straining to push this waterlogged tub—and soon we should expect either a rain of heavy ammunition or perhaps some kind of boarding party. If I were a Marko-knowing millionaire, I'd start with the long-range option.

So now it's time to relocate to warmer climes, Louis. To the kitchen! It's a poor hiding place for any length of time, but blissfully warmer than this arctic place, and the side entrance is mere inches from the lifeboat. We only need to wait for that moment when Marko is too distracted to care about us—specifically, to care about shooting at us. When the bombs fall, we rise.

Can you stand, Louis? Here, lean on me. We're taking a short trip—oh, of course, your legs are still tied. How rude of me. I'll cut you free upstairs, but ... no, you couldn't stand anyway, could you? Poor man. Over the shoulder, then. Don't worry, it's a short distance, and I contain the strength of millions.

Welcome to my kitchen, Louis. Here is where I perform miracles. But for Christ's sake, stop your coughing—the Captain could hear you, he's right outside! You've been a master of silence all evening, please don't ruin your record now. Lean on me, let's step around this mess on the floor. Don't dent your brain on the overhanging pans.

Hear those footsteps? He's pacing the ship, muttering. But he doesn't know we're here. Let's keep it that way, Louis. Why is he away from the wheelhouse? I don't even dare peek through those swinging doors. He could barge in demanding breakfast, lunch or dinner at any hour, any moment.

We need to hide you. Where will we? The reach-in freezer is just about the right size ... no, blast it, it's right by the doors, he'll see it swinging open. The Vulcan could fit you, it's a double-stack convection job ... but I'd have to pull all the racks, that would make a racket and an obvious clue. Also there are temperature-regulation issues—I burn myself on it almost daily.

Aha—I've got just the thing! Here, lean a moment. I need to curl you up into a ball, Louis, just for a little while. Now up ... and down ... and into the pot you go. Two hundred quarts, my largest. I think if you tuck your head I can just about close the lid ... yes, perfect. Who would think to glance inside?

How's that? Comfy? It's the very same pot you peeked into this morning, actually. Surgical stainless steel. This genre of cuisine has required a number of oversized implements. I've reduced an entire baboon to stock in this pot. Most recently we made Consommé Pandora, a slow and careful reduction of egg, ex-wife and mirepoix; there may still be a thin layer clinging to the sides. Sorry, nothing's as clean as it should be today.

Peekaboo! Hello, look at you, fit to parboil! I'm seized by the urge to peel some onions.

Kidding! Just kidding, Louis! Please pardon my bad jokes. We'll leave off the lid for now. Thank you for your continued patience with our peculiar predicament.

Who is he talking to out there?

Ah yes: Salome. He talks to Salome, still. Not that she listens.

There is the crux, you know; there is the cheese in the trap. One could lay it all on Salome, but still I point the finger at Marko: if only he had brought back any other sommelier from Paris than Salome, everything on this boat would still be orderly and hospitable. The millionaires would be out there in the dining room munching away at themselves, you and I would be whole and healthy and the world would be our oyster. And some other wine steward, some knowledgeable and polite older gentleman perhaps, not so beautiful, not so trusting, certainly not with a heart of pure charity and joy, would open this next bottle for us.

But instead it falls to me. '98 Châteauneuf, I presume you approve. It'll get your blood up, soothe your throat, help you with that wracking cough, ease your general pain. I'm fresh out of glasses, but here, have a sip from the bottle and tell me if it's gone off. Try not to dribble on the manuscript.

Oh, Salome, Salome, Salome ... she was something else, Louis, something for the heart and eyes. Truly she did not belong here, but was she ever unhappy?

I blame myself as well. I informed Marko, nine months ago, that we'd need more help. The first tremors of the Avalanche were rattling, our reservation book was thickening with commitments. There was no choice but to add staff.

Marko wasn't having it at all. Too risky, with our great boatload of secrets. I told him: get me someone just for wine and salads, to stock the pantry and work with the suppliers who boat out here once a week with our shopping. He'll never be in the kitchen, he'll never go downstairs. I will simply not allow it. It will be a shooting offense.

Marko hated the idea, but—we were killing ourselves! We used local boys for the dining room staff, trainable enough when you could find one without birth defects, but unreliable, un-punctual and above all indiscreet—far too curious. I told Marko: we need a professional with discipline and a good sense of boundaries. We will keep him contained. If he ever does cross the line and make a dangerous discovery, where can he go? What can he do?

Marko resisted, stonewalled—for a while just bringing up the issue drove him into a rage—but a first class restaurateur needs to do things like this if he wants to please millionaires. I'm no oneologist, Louis: I'm ashamed to say my knowledge is not half what it should be. My obsessions have been in other areas. We were sorely lacking in wine authority, and wine is the very first things millionaires judge: how old, how expensive, how dusty the label.

Marko fumed, stamped, screamed, struck and stabbed. But then, oddly enough, after going off on one of his home excursions—he goes home to Serbia twice a year to pay tribute to his mafioso uncles, launder his money and hurt various people— but this time he returned with four crates of wine and one doe-eyed waif on top.

Salome: an Italian girl, raised in Tuscany, with olive skin and curly jet-black hair that bobbed like a cluster of grapes. She was the daughter of a prosperous vintner, she studied cuisine at Le Ferrandi and then travelled the world, working at various wineries. She lived and breathed wine—vines were like children to her. She'd tasted everything, she knew everyone, and when she discussed wine with our more educated guests she enchanted them all with her esoteric knowledge and her fierce laughter.

A beautiful woman in the dining room who knows everything about wine and can weave stories around it—this is restaurant gold, Louis! This is a secret weapon, this is the perfect sommelier. She was a genius of wine, and thoroughly competent in every other job we gave her. We paid her well, but Louis, she could have earned just as much in any fine restaurant on earth.

In fact, I believe now that Marko poached her out from under the head chef at Les Profiteroles in the 13th arrondissement. I believe he wooed her with tales of exotic island living, of the needy Cristobos and the good work we were doing. I believe she was hungry for experience, tired of cities, happier out in the open under the sun.

She took up residence in a simple hut on the island, far from this foolish old men's boat. She got to know the locals, volunteered on her free days at the mangy little hospital shack there, caring for the many deformed Cristobo children. Until the last two months she seemed quite happy in our tiny paradise.

I don't presume to understand her relationship with Marko; suffice it to say that she got to know a very different side of him from the one you and I have met. Strong, quick and devious as he is, he exudes a certain aura of menace and excitement to which some women are drawn—but I credit Salome with more intelligence. And like any beautiful, intelligent young woman, she had some skill in the manipulation of men. I know they wanted things from one another, I know they were both cunning and patient in their strategies. I never saw them kiss, but I assumed certain things went on. We all did.

Except: as time wore on here in our little boat, as Salome became part of the efficient running of things, as our business boomed and our notoriety grew and the Avalanche washed over us and we beat it back, I believe Salome, quite naturally, became curious.

And then Marko became furious. Something changed between the two of them several months ago, all in a day. There was a moment when I feared the worst—I was so fond of her, Louis! She brought such beauty and light into an old man's ragged world—but no, rather than catastrophe it led to some unspoken realignment. Whatever privacies might have gone on between them, they went on no longer. Salome just did her job, pocketed her pay, and spent more and more time on the most distant parts of the island.

Marko, for his part, refused ever to lash out at her—a remarkable bit of restraint for our Marko! But for him, the game had not yet ended. I felt a change, though: an uptick in his mercurial nature, his little fits and rants and stabbings. And he began to work out his frustrations on the millionaires in ways that were unpleasant to watch and, from a strictly culinary standpoint, totally unnecessary.

Chilly as Salome grew toward Marko, she never held any kind of grudge against me. Early on I convinced her that I was a certain kind of dangerous man, a paranoid genius, and that any attempt to pry into the secrets of my kitchen would lead to dismissal at the very least. She respected my boundaries admirably, and even under the often crushing stress of our success we never bickered, she never contradicted me, I never gave her decisions a second guess. When mistakes happened in the procurement she immediately fixed them. She was a great talent, our Salome. In the late relaxing hour after doors are shut, chairs are put on tables and counters are wiped down, she sometimes smiled at me, embraced me once or twice.

And I assure you, Louis: I was good! I never once touched her, I never *dreamed* of touching her. The scent of her, the look of her, the softness of her skin would make a crocodile weep. But never once did I so much as salivate in her presence. I promise you, Louis. You would have been proud of me.

So she continued to work her magic on the millionaires. The way she held their attention you'd think she was profit incarnate. And I believe they fascinated her as well—they do cut a rough charming figure, our rich pirates, our well-armed yachtsmen. She wanted to know all about them, especially the more handsome ones.

I believe Salome was beginning to visualize herself elsewhere. I think she was just waiting for the right millionaire, and she would have left us without so much as a note. I saw it, Marko saw it too.

As did our best customer, Mr. Hazmat. They were on very comfortable terms, he and she; he stayed late to chat with her when the rush let up, ordering bottle after bottle of fine champagne. He had a deepening interest in wine, and plied her with questions about what to drink in all the beautiful places he regularly visited. Sometimes he, or one of his men, would accompany her home after closing—as if any place on Cristobal Minor was more dangerous than this boat. Or perhaps they went elsewhere; I'm told Mr. Hazmat's yacht is equipped with a hot tub, and decorated with a fine collection of etchings.

What else did Marko expect, luring an innocent like Salome into a den of cannibals and millionaires? What else could have happened? I hope he didn't imagine he'd marry her, settle down with her, make little cannibals.

No, I imagine what Marko planned is exactly what happened. Albeit with a twist.

And with that twist, the world is turned against us. The Cristobos, whose dying island we reanimated: they loved Salome, simply adored her. She was their Evita, and now they demand vengeance and the ownership of her remains. The millionaires whose peculiar needs we so fittingly served: they loved her too, and simply can't believe what's happened. Everybody loved Salome—Louis, I loved her too! Taking her downstairs was the hardest thing I've ever done. Holding her down, whispering as she screamed, watching Marko as he tore out her—

Shh! Listen. It's him again. Do you hear him whimpering? Marko loved Salome most of all, and still does—that's why he's still talking to her now: pacing the decks with her in hand, peering into her ghastly eyes, apologizing to her numb dead ears, stroking the hair on her severed head. He's saying he'll change, he's promising her a new beginning, even as he's digesting a roast of her buttocks and inner thighs.

It's a unique sort of love, our Marko's—but so sincere!

You see, Louis? This is why I've got to quit. Not because we're shut down and sinking, though we are. Not because Marko has become hard to work with, though "hard" is hardly the word. And absolutely not that I shouldn't eat the delicious, selfish, healthful, parasitic, vitamin-rich bastard millionaires—or that I don't want to! I absolutely should, and do.

But I've done a terrible thing.

I vowed to myself: I will eat millionaires, only, exclusively. As long as I only eat millionaires, I can hold up my head, I can smile, I can live with myself. Better yet, I'll recruit others to join me in this feast! Together we will make the world a better, fairer place. This old world of ours, Louis, is so sad and worn, besieged and exploited, so desperate for my help! What a hero I was! Married to my quest, guided by a star, sustained by an inner light.

But Salome was no millionaire. Tasting her, my fire went out. I am plunged back into an old familiar darkness, where right and wrong escape me. I'm no longer a man, not even an animal. I'm just a puppet of hunger, a gut slave.

Although she was delicious, she did not agree with me.

And Marko? Listen to him, crying on the deck as gunships swarm around, positioning themselves like golfers on the green. He's like a child who's eaten his mother. He's done himself in and he knows it—there's no one else to blame. The ultimate downfall, the king dethroned—

—Cunting dickfucks.

—Marko!

—The dickfuckers. The dickfucking cows. Running out on me with their pricks around their nuts like fancy neckties. Fancy cunts, not worth their weight in shit. Tasty though. Who are you talking to, André?

—Marko, you startled me. What's happening, where are we going? What's the plan?

—André ... she's hungry.

—This is hardly the time, Marko! Don't you know we're sinking?

—Salome wants supper, André. Something to stick to her ribs. Only the best, André. Don't let her down. Only the best for our lady, am I right? What's in the pot?

—It's ... it was going to be a ragoût, of our visitor, that gentleman from earlier. The man in question. But I'm only just getting started.

—Hardly the time, André. Hardly the time.

—Marko, what's going to happen? You're bleeding, look at you—

—We're going home, André. Home to Bečići until this all blows over. Everything's upside-down since I left, dickfuckers are running around calling me names. There's work to do. And after that's sorted, Salome's going to marry me. She's going to meet my one-toothed granny and all my cousins and uncles. "Marko made his nut," that's what they'll see her and say. And a white dress, and presents in shiny paper, and a great big house on the cliff. All of that shit. She's so fucking pretty. Isn't she, André? Isn't she? Like those paintings you showed me in Berlin, but she's real.

—Marko ... I hear gunfire. Rockets.

—I heard you talking, André. Whom to, is what I'm wondering.

—You, Marko! I'm talking to you.

—Shut up! You're a prissy little monkey, André! Oh, but *they're* scared of you though. Those cows, those dickfucking cows, they think *you're* the boogeyman who's going to come and eat them. Limp little you. You even frightened Mister Guns and

Ammo. The prissy Persian faggot. All those luxury snobdicks. Soft stupid cows.

—Marko?

—Cows with fucking guns, André! We're surrounded. My cuntfucking breakfast is pointing guns at me! Don't they know who's the biggest asshole in this ocean? Oh, we'll eat bloody rare tonight, André! Those pontooned pricks don't know whom with which they're fucking.

—Marko, listen to the engines. They're ripping themselves apart. We'll be dead in the water soon.

—Shut up! We're on our fucking way to fucking Bečići! Did I tell you about the house, André? There's pictures somewhere. On the tip of Zavata, sticking into the bay, owning the fucking Mediterranean like a cock on a whore's nose. It's almost built, I've got a gang of gypsies tiling the roof of it right now. With fucking hundred dollar bills as far as I can tell. That house better be built with solid gold nails, what it's fucking costing me. We'll go stay there a while. You can cook something soft for Grannie. We'll fry up a few of those gypsy cuntholes, make them eat their hundred dollar tiles. Ripping me off. Fucking with Marko.

—Marko, Mr. Hazmat's out there and he's holding all the cards ... you used to be so good at talking to him—

—I will bite out his goddamn heart! The shit he did, I'm going to yank that fucker's guts one at a time, hang them around his neck like a, like a fucking medal! That's the medal you win for fucking with Marko. Nobody fucks with Marko. Even Salome ... so pretty ... but she had me on a fucking leash, like a toy dog strapped to a millionaire's wife! And you don't, you don't do that. To Marko. You don't! That just doesn't go down. It sticks in the throat, right here. And I did tell her I was sorry, André, I said as much, didn't I? You heard me fucking tell her and it's her fault, she did it to herself. By the fucking. The fucking with Marko! The fucking with Marko that just isn't done, am I right?

—Okay, yes! Yes of course, absolutely, never more so, Marko. But you've just reminded me: perhaps I should have a look at the lifeboat, you know? Just in case we might need it soon.

—Shut up! I'm right! I'm Marko! And Salome ... now Salome is all better. Isn't she? Now she's settled down. Now she's perfect. Except ... except she's crying, André. She's sad, because now everybody's so nosy. Every cunting dickfuck in the ocean wants to fuck with Marko now. That makes her sad. And you, André. You make her very fucking depressed today. Why the fuck, André?

—Me? What? Sorry?

—Salome's crying, André. She says you've let us down. She says you're hiding something. What is she talking about, André?

—I swear upon my mother's grave I haven't a clue.

—I smell him. The little man with the pens.

—Oh, yes ... yes Marko, but I just told you, he's in the pot.

—Shouldn't you turn the heat on then?

—The heat? Fine, okay, there, you see? The heat is goddamn *on*, Marko! Satisfied? Now get a grip! Millionaires are about to torpedo us in the open sea! Is that not hot enough? Why, why do you choose *this* of any moment to abandon all your responsibilities, barge in to *my* kitchen and try to tell *me* how to do my job? This is Quebec Ragoût De Pattes et Avant-Bras, you philistine! Not some—OW!

—Turn it up, André. All the way.

—Aaagh! Oh God oh God oh God!

—I want to smell him burning.

—Yes! Okay! Oh God, stop it, Marko! They're shooting at us!

—The bullets are my problem, André. Say it.

—OW! Yes! The bullets! They're your problem!

—Your problem is Marko.

—My problem is Marko! Please put down the grapefruit spoon!

—You're very sorry for talking back to me. Never will you do it again.

—Absolutely never! Very sorry!

—Shut up!

— ...

—Forget it, it doesn't matter.

— ...

—We'll just eat you. You and the little man, yes. Me and Salome are going to eat the shit out of both of you.

—But but but but—do you hear that whistling? Something's coming, Marko!

—Shut up and get in the pot. Salome's hungry.

—You can't even cook, Marko! Listen to that!

—GET! IN! THE! POT!

—Marko, it's missiles ...

Sleep sweetly, Louis.

There's something about a boat, isn't there? Even a humble inflatable such as this one. It cradles one softly like a mother and lulls even the most troubled hearts to sleep.

Such peace, now. The water placid all around us, nothing on the horizon but the sculpted stern of that yacht towing us, and the infinite V of its radiating wake. The sun is low in the sky, sandwiched in that poignant position between the clouds and the water. After all I've just witnessed, Louis, I am drained, wiped, dry. I'm ready to join you.

Sleep, dearest friend. You've done well—everything you set out to achieve has been accomplished, laid at your feet like a birthday present. A lifetime of integrity, honesty and curiosity has rewarded you well. You've won.

It's only a pity, Louis, that your powerful eyes were closed for that last remarkable scene! My God, the drama! How the missiles ripped apart the kitchen! A landslide of pots, pans and cutlery! How I dragged you out of there, up the listing deck to the lifeboats. Marko running to the wheelhouse, screaming epithets on the radio and blasting away at the yachts, with the engines sputtering and the black clouds of burnt oil roiling from holes in the deck. How he spun that massive cannon in all directions, lobbing wild explosions across the water, trying with all his best persuasion to scare a hole in their blockade as they circled for the kill, dodging and parrying with their ultra-powerful millionaire motors, their seasoned crews, their many expensive guns.

They had every advantage, really. Marko face to face is an unstoppable force, but at the helm of a listing, burning, wounded fishery surrounded by sleek pleasure craft, he was just a wounded whale in a pod of orcas.

I'm proud of you, Louis: you waited with utmost patience for the moment of truth—and it came, as I promised it would. I only wish it would have come sooner. If we'd gotten away earlier I might still have rowed us back to Cristobal Minor and made good on my promise of rescue.

But then I would never have witnessed the final battle, the one through which you slept: Mr. Hazmat's mighty gunship pulling in front of us, and Marko punishing the engines, wrestling the wheel to keep our bearing as he made to ram!

Mr. Hazmat accepted the challenge and charged straight at us. The bow of his craft came on us like an axe as I wrestled with the lifeboat boom. One of his many cannons blew apart my dining room, knives and forks and broken glass shot in all directions— and Marko charged screaming from the wheelhouse with a cleaver in one hand and Salome's head by the hair in the other, running up the bow as if to stab the attacking ship in the face.

I'll say this about Hazmat: for a millionaire, he has a wicked sense of humor. Armed as he was with every known surface-to-surface weapon, every caliber of ammunition, every bomb and knife, which one do you think he used, Louis, to deal the final blow? A harpoon. The large complicated gunrack on his very foremost bit of deck is apparently the harpoon cannon he uses to hunt whales.

The last I saw our Marko he was still alive: impaled amidships against the door of the wheelhouse as the crushing bow of Hazmat's yacht tore through our decks like a hatchet through a calf's head. Then, l'Arche, and all its remarkable cargo (ourselves included) scattered on the sea. So finely shattered it no longer resembled a ship at all, just an interesting flotilla of jetsam.

Curiously, some of the cargo from the cooler chose to float. Poultry, mostly, but also those cuts of giraffe neck—impossible to get rid of, that stuff. The relative buoyancy of different meats, I suppose, is a worthwhile study; some food scientist would have liked to gather that data. But the eels left no time for that—they made a fierce frenzy of it, thrashing and gnashing with their snapping jaws and tiny eyes. The ocean simmered with them, quivering with angry engergy. I dare say it was the same school of eels from the harbor—they must have followed the boat, drawn by the smell of us or somehow sensing the golden opportunity. It's what they've dreamed of, if eels have dreams.

But that will be the final restaurant meal for those eels. There will be no more bones for the Cristobo crabs, and no more sausages for the Cristobo orphans. No more reason, in fact, for yachtsmen or anyone else to moor there. Native Crafts, as a growth industry, are over.

And I have cooked my last three star millionaire meal, Louis. You have won, indeed. Where could I go? How could I follow this success? What more can I prove? No, I am retired, officially. As the greatest chef of the New Food, I bequeath the world of cuisine my thanks, my adoration, and of course my manuscript, still on your delicious person. When Mr. Hazmat finally reels in what remains of us out of here, he'll have to be my editor. I dearly hope he enjoys it.

Will he? He's a curious man, Hazmat, and he's always loved my cooking. I wish he wouldn't allow his grudge with Marko to spill over on our relations. I think it was him I spied earlier, smoking a cigar and peering at us from the brass railing. It's hard to be sure, with this towline so long.

But there is another man watching, I can see him well. His tall paper hat tilts at us against the darkening sky, and the twilight glints against that little paring knife of his. I know him, Louis. His name is Jesse Bruno, a jealous little galley slave. Former proprietor of that hideous tofu joint Spice Nine, he is currently employed as the personal chef to Mr. Hazmat. On those nights when Hazmat moored his yacht beside us to dine, I often spied Bruno leering at us from the deck like a spurned lover. Cuisine is a small world, and chefs can be so very petty.

Now there's a man who really ought to read my book. I wonder what he's waiting for. How long does he intend to keep us dangling here?

Feh. It doesn't concern me in the least. My work is done. And I'm well-supplied for a journey of any length.

It's such a pity you've died, Louis. I still have so many questions ... the first and foremost being, are you sure you're not a millionaire? As last meals go, you have given me the ultimate. This calf of yours, it's sweet as candy, salty as the sea, and the texture spreads like a warm blanket in the mouth. I only wish I had it in my kitchen—braised in fat from your thigh, the sugars would caramelize and the marbling would glisten. Deglazed with sherry and a shallot you'd make a king's gravy. And that unique flavor of yours, hinted at in your hands, is here in abundance, an earthy, nutty marinade—metallic, slightly, but not unpleasantly so. Earthy like rust, like fungus. You've shown me a brand new flavor, Louis, and that is the finest gift a chef could ask for.

Gift: now there's a funny word. It's the English word for a present, but as you probably know, Louis, it's also the German word for a poison. This flavor in you ... I thought perhaps arsenic, but no. That would be too simple. You're such a sophisticate,

Louis, I'm sure you studied and consulted many mystified doctors and puzzled chemists, always hinting at your goal while never admitting it. I'm sure you personally tasted various poisons at some microscopic dilution, or had others taste them for you—oh, there's an eerie thought, Louis, you old cad! But your approach, whatever it was, undoubtably succeeded: you identified the very perfect compound. It kills slowly but certainly, suffuses the tissues of the entire body, and leaves no unpleasant aftertaste in the flesh, no alarming fingerprint to tip off your victim—in fact, it renders human flesh that much more appealing! Louis De Gustibus, scholar of flavor, historian of food, protector of diners everywhere, if there is a perfect poison to kill a cannibal, I trust you to find it.

And I'm flattered, Louis. You know, it was hardly necessary. I would have eaten you anyway, despite any lingering bitterness. I can now feel, in the very base of my lungs, the wet germ of that characteristic cough you had—the first, I'm sure, of many symptoms I will recognize—but I have no regrets. You are, I declare, the finest meal of my life. And I have eaten well indeed.

I found your letter, Louis. You put it in the correct place, the location just beside the hip where the long femur is severed from the coccyx. But you took a risk, I think—what if we'd broken you completely down before cooking you? Had I guessed your plan, might I have declined your dinner invitation?

Then again, probably not. I'm a hungry man, Louis, and I hate to waste good food.

So sleep, my dear friend. It's been an ideal evening. Thank you for knowing me, appreciating me, and indeed for trying so hard to reform me. You could have had me strung up at any time, Louis. You knew enough, the police would have teased out the rest. When you confronted me at La Tartine I thought I was undone, but you granted me an extension, a last chance, and I made the most of it. Thank you.

You and I are lovers, Louis—lovers in food. The chef and the gourmet, the flower and the bee. I'm exquisitely happy with the ending you've given me, Louis. A hero's death for both of us. See you in Valhalla, eh? Or in some golden flying mansion, or some fiery pit? Who knows if there are millionaires in Heaven, Louis, but I thoroughly expect to see them in Hell. But no matter where my soul and I are next transmitted, I will apply my humble skills where they are appreciated.

My last decision, then, concerns this manuscript. Can I trust this important document to millionaires? I'm thinking not. Perhaps Jesse Bruno would crib my recipes, but the rest? Anathema. The very idea of it reaching a wide audience ought to terrify them. Mr. Hazmat is no fool, he's a millionaire's millionaire. He protects his own.

So, Louis, I am now curling up the pages into little tubes just narrow enough to fit through the neck of this, our last bottle. The finest item from our cellar, Louis: a 1916 jeroboam of Roederer's Cristal—from the private cellars of Tsar Nicholas the Second, in his very last year of patronage before the Bolshevik flood. A bottle older than us, Louis, older than our parents perhaps. Wine from an era less tainted by the smell of money. A cork that has lasted close to one hundred years and will, I think, last one hundred more. Corks were stronger then, from stouter trees, and the bottle, you know, is real leaded glass, hand-blown by a master. Transparent, so Nicholas could hold it to the light and be certain it contained no poison, no bombs—hence the name Cristal. If this bottle could endure what history wrought through Europe in the twentieth century, then it's the perfect vessel to protect my message, which I think will only improve with age.

Buoyed with air it will drift on the sea for who knows how many years. It may be discovered on a beach, or in the belly of a whale. It may fall into the gravity of the Great Pacific Gyre, that huge dump in the ocean that slowly burns, but one day I know this bottle will be found and opened. It's a '16 Cristal, after all! In some future place, in some advanced version of our current sorry state of world affairs, someone will receive this advice, and act upon it.

That's assuming, of course, that millionaires will still be a problem in the future. But I can hardly doubt it—as long as there's poverty, there will be millionaires.

September 12, 2009

My dear André,

I must write this down because I've lost my voice to tumors, in my brain and elsewhere. My doctors are poor liars who insist that I might recover, given this clinic or that procedure. But I have chosen instead to occupy my remaining days in this blessed world with the completion of unfinished business, and no outstanding issue presses heavier on my heart that the problem of what to do with you. So perhaps it's best that I compose my intentions now, later to present them to you upon a silver tray with something like that same suave affectation of innocence with which you've offered up so many of your unholy meals.

I have recently received damning reports from a woman I trust. But you will not read this letter until I have personally confirmed the worst: that you have returned to your rotten, psychopathic patterns; that the goodness I once detected in your heart has drowned in the tremendous and ravenous evil there; that you have broken your solemn oath, sworn to me upon our Savior's cross; and that you have forgotten certain consequences, or come to believe you can evade them. You cannot.

Therefore: I sentence you, André, to death. There is no pleasure in it. I do it for the safety of humanity in general. Certain wrongs are absolute. My responsibility in this matter is clear. It pains me terribly, but it also closes the last chapter in a troubling, ambiguous story that has robbed me of peace for a long time.

I shall not negotiate. You've used up all my mercy. I can only express my sincere regret that all my less drastic solutions have failed. Know that whatever cosmic judgement waits for you, André, it also waits for me. Because I have made you my responsibility, I am complicit in your murders, and it sickens me. I must make amends.

However, if another world exists after this one, perhaps its metaphysics will allow us the luxury of that simple friendship we both desired so strongly. I have found many traits to admire in you, André, but many more to fear.

Adieu, for now,
-Louis D.

ABOUT THE AUTHOR

Mykle Hansen only eats vegetables that died peacefully in their sleep. He is the author of the bizarro novel HELP! A BEAR IS EATING ME! and the rude collection RAMPAGING FUCK-ERS OF EVERYTHING ON THE CRAZY SHITTING PLANET OF THE VOMIT ATMO-SPHERE. He resides in Portland, Oregon with his delicious wife, tasty daughter and beloved chickens. He promises this is his last book about cannibalism.

Bizarro books

CATALOG   SPRING 2010

Bizarro Books publishes under the following imprints:

www.rawdogscreamingpress.com

www.eraserheadpress.com

www.afterbirthbooks.com

www.swallowdownpress.com

For all your Bizarro needs visit:

WWW.BIZARROCENTRAL.COM

Introduce yourselves to the bizarro genre and all of its authors with the Bizarro Starter Kit series. Each volume features short novels and short stories by ten of the leading bizarro authors, designed to give you a perfect sampling of the genre for only $5 plus shipping.

BB-0X1
"The Bizarro Starter Kit"
(Orange)

Featuring D. Harlan Wilson, Carlton Mellick III, Jeremy Robert Johnson, Kevin L Donihe, Gina Ranalli, Andre Duza, Vincent W. Sakowski, Steve Beard, John Edward Lawson, and Bruce Taylor.

236 pages $5

BB-0X2
"The Bizarro Starter Kit"
(Blue)

Featuring Ray Fracalossy, Jeremy C. Shipp, Jordan Krall, Mykle Hansen, Andersen Prunty, Eckhard Gerdes, Bradley Sands, Steve Aylett, Christian TeBordo, and Tony Rauch.

244 pages $5

BB-001"The Kafka Effekt" D. Harlan Wilson - A collection of forty-four irreal short stories loosely written in the vein of Franz Kafka, with more than a pinch of William S. Burroughs sprinkled on top. **211 pages $14**

BB-002 "Satan Burger" Carlton Mellick III - The cult novel that put Carlton Mellick III on the map ... Six punks get jobs at a fast food restaurant owned by the devil in a city violently overpopulated by surreal alien cultures. **236 pages $14**

BB-003 "Some Things Are Better Left Unplugged" Vincent Sakwoski - Join The Man and his Nemesis, the obese tabby, for a nightmare roller coaster ride into this postmodern fantasy. **152 pages $10**

BB-004 "Shall We Gather At the Garden?" Kevin L Donihe - Donihe's Debut novel. Midgets take over the world, The Church of Lionel Richie vs. The Church of the Byrds, plant porn and more! **244 pages $14**

BB-005 "Razor Wire Pubic Hair" Carlton Mellick III - A genderless humandildo is purchased by a razor dominatrix and brought into her nightmarish world of bizarre sex and mutilation. **176 pages $11**

BB-006 "Stranger on the Loose" D. Harlan Wilson - The fiction of Wilson's 2nd collection is planted in the soil of normalcy, but what grows out of that soil is a dark, witty, otherworldly jungle... **228 pages $14**

BB-007 "The Baby Jesus Butt Plug" Carlton Mellick III - Using clones of the Baby Jesus for anal sex will be the hip sex fetish of the future. **92 pages $10**

BB-008 "Fishyfleshed" Carlton Mellick III - The world of the past is an illogical flatland lacking in dimension and color, a sick-scape of crispy squid people wandering the desert for no apparent reason. **260 pages $14**

BB-009 **"Dead Bitch Army" Andre Duza** - Step into a world filled with racist teenagers, cannibals, 100 warped Uncle Sams, automobiles with razor-sharp teeth, living graffiti, and a pissed-off zombie bitch out for revenge. **344 pages $16**

BB-010 **"The Menstruating Mall" Carlton Mellick III** - "The Breakfast Club meets Chopping Mall as directed by David Lynch." - Brian Keene **212 pages $12**

BB-011 **"Angel Dust Apocalypse" Jeremy Robert Johnson** - Meth-heads, man-made monsters, and murderous Neo-Nazis. "Seriously amazing short stories..." - Chuck Palahniuk, author of Fight Club **184 pages $11**

BB-012 **"Ocean of Lard" Kevin L Donihe / Carlton Mellick III** - A parody of those old Choose Your Own Adventure kid's books about some very odd pirates sailing on a sea made of animal fat. **176 pages $12**

BB-013 **"Last Burn in Hell" John Edward Lawson** - From his lurid angst-affair with a lesbian music diva to his ascendance as unlikely pop icon the one constant for Kenrick Brimley, official state prison gigolo, is he's got no clue what he's doing. **172 pages $14**

BB-014 **"Tangerinephant" Kevin Dole 2** - TV-obsessed aliens have abducted Michael Tangerinephant in this bizarro combination of science fiction, satire, and surrealism. **164 pages $11**

BB-015 **"Foop!" Chris Genoa** - Strange happenings are going on at Dactyl, Inc, the world's first and only time travel tourism company.

"A surreal pie in the face!" - Christopher Moore **300 pages $14**

BB-016 **"Spider Pie" Alyssa Sturgill** - A one-way trip down a rabbit hole inhabited by sexual deviants and friendly monsters, fairytale beginnings and hideous endings. **104 pages $11**

BB-017 "The Unauthorized Woman" Efrem Emerson - Enter the world of the inner freak, a landscape populated by the pre-dead and morticioners, by cockroaches and 300-lb robots. **104 pages $11**

BB-018 "Fugue XXIX" Forrest Aguirre - Tales from the fringe of speculative literary fiction where innovative minds dream up the future's uncharted territories while mining forgotten treasures of the past. **220 pages $16**

BB-019 "Pocket Full of Loose Razorblades" John Edward Lawson - A collection of dark bizarro stories. From a giant rectum to a foot-fungus factory to a girl with a biforked tongue. **190 pages $13**

BB-020 "Punk Land" Carlton Mellick III - In the punk version of Heaven, the anarchist utopia is threatened by corporate fascism and only Goblin, Mortician's sperm, and a blue-mohawked female assassin named Shark Girl can stop them. **284 pages $15**

BB-021 "Pseudo-City" D. Harlan Wilson - Pseudo-City exposes what waits in the bathroom stall, under the manhole cover and in the corporate boardroom, all in a way that can only be described as mind-bogglingly irreal. **220 pages $16**

BB-022 "Kafka's Uncle and Other Strange Tales" Bruce Taylor - Anslenot and his giant tarantula (tormentor? fri-end?) wander a desecrated world in this novel and collection of stories from Mr. Magic Realism Himself. **348 pages $17**

BB-023 "Sex and Death In Television Town" Carlton Mellick III - In the old west, a gang of hermaphrodite gunslingers take refuge from a demon plague in Telos: a town where its citizens have televisions instead of heads. **184 pages $12**

BB-024 "It Came From Below The Belt" Bradley Sands - What can Grover Goldstein do when his severed, sentient penis forces him to return to high school and help it win the presidential election? **204 pages $13**

BB-025 **"Sick: An Anthology of Illness" John Lawson, editor** - These Sick stories are horrendous and hilarious dissections of creative minds on the scalpel's edge. **296 pages $16**

BB-026 **"Tempting Disaster" John Lawson, editor** - A shocking and alluring anthology from the fringe that examines our culture's obsession with taboos. **260 pages $16**

BB-027 **"Siren Promised" Jeremy Robert Johnson & Alan M Clark** - Nominated for the Bram Stoker Award. A potent mix of bad drugs, bad dreams, brutal bad guys, and surreal/incredible art by Alan M. Clark. **190 pages $13**

BB-028 **"Chemical Gardens" Gina Ranalli** - Ro and punk band Green is the Enemy find Kreepkins, a surfer-dude warlock, a vengeful demon, and a Metal Priestess in their way as they try to escape an underground nightmare. **188 pages $13**

BB-029 **"Jesus Freaks" Andre Duza** - For God so loved the world that he gave his only two begotten sons… and a few million zombies. **400 pages $16**

BB-030 **"Grape City" Kevin L. Donihe** - More Donihe-style comedic bizarro about a demon named Charles who is forced to work a minimum wage job on Earth after Hell goes out of business. **108 pages $10**

BB-031 **"Sea of the Patchwork Cats" Carlton Mellick III** - A quiet dreamlike tale set in the ashes of the human race. For Mellick enthusiasts who also adore The Twilight Zone. **112 pages $10**

BB-032 **"Extinction Journals" Jeremy Robert Johnson** - An uncanny voyage across a newly nuclear America where one man must confront the problems associated with loneliness, insane dieties, radiation, love, and an ever-evolving cockroach suit with a mind of its own. **104 pages $10**

BB-033 **"Meat Puppet Cabaret" Steve Beard** - At last! The secret connection between Jack the Ripper and Princess Diana's death revealed! **240 pages $16 / $30**

BB-034 **"The Greatest Fucking Moment in Sports" Kevin L. Donihe** - In the tradition of the surreal anti-sitcom Get A Life comes a tale of triumph and agape love from the master of comedic bizarro. **108 pages $10**

BB-035 **"The Troublesome Amputee" John Edward Lawson** - Disturbing verse from a man who truly believes nothing is sacred and intends to prove it. **104 pages $9**

BB-036 **"Deity" Vic Mudd** - God (who doesn't like to be called "God") comes down to a typical, suburban, Ohio family for a little vacation—but it doesn't turn out to be as relaxing as He had hoped it would be... **168 pages $12**

BB-037 **"The Haunted Vagina" Carlton Mellick III** - It's difficult to love a woman whose vagina is a gateway to the world of the dead. **132 pages $10**

BB-038 **"Tales from the Vinegar Wasteland" Ray Fracalossy** - Witness: a man is slowly losing his face, a neighbor who periodically screams out for no apparent reason, and a house with a room that doesn't actually exist. **240 pages $14**

BB-039 **"Suicide Girls in the Afterlife" Gina Ranalli** - After Pogue commits suicide, she unexpectedly finds herself an unwilling "guest" at a hotel in the Afterlife, where she meets a group of bizarre characters, including a goth Satan, a hippie Jesus, and an alien-human hybrid. **100 pages $9**

BB-040 **"And Your Point Is?" Steve Aylett** - In this follow-up to LINT multiple authors provide critical commentary and essays about Jeff Lint's mind-bending literature. **104 pages $11**

BB-041 **"Not Quite One of the Boys" Vincent Sakowski** - While drug-dealer Maxi drinks with Dante in purgatory, God and Satan play a little tri-level chess and do a little bargaining over his business partner, Vinnie, who is still left on earth. **220 pages $14**

BB-042 **"Teeth and Tongue Landscape" Carlton Mellick III** - On a planet made out of meat, a socially-obsessive monophobic man tries to find his place amongst the strange creatures and communities that he comes across. **110 pages $10**

BB-043 **"War Slut" Carlton Mellick III** - Part "1984," part "Waiting for Godot," and part action horror video game adaptation of John Carpenter's "The Thing." **116 pages $10**

BB-044 **"All Encompassing Trip" Nicole Del Sesto** - In a world where coffee is no longer available, the only television shows are reality TV re-runs, and the animals are talking back, Nikki, Amber and a singing Coyote in a do-rag are out to restore the light **308 pages $15**

BB-045 **"Dr. Identity" D. Harlan Wilson** - Follow the Dystopian Duo on a killing spree of epic proportions through the irreal postcapitalist city of Bliptown where time ticks sideways, artificial Bug-Eyed Monsters punish citizens for consumer-capitalist lethargy, and ultraviolence is as essential as a daily multivitamin. **208 pages $15**

BB-046 **"The Million-Year Centipede" Eckhard Gerdes** - Wakelin, frontman for 'The Hinge,' wrote a poem so prophetic that to ignore it dooms a person to drown in blood. **130 pages $12**

BB-047 **"Sausagey Santa" Carlton Mellick III** - A bizarro Christmas tale featuring Santa as a piratey mutant with a body made of sausages. 124 pages $10

BB-048 **"Misadventures in a Thumbnail Universe" Vincent Sakowski** - Dive deep into the surreal and satirical realms of neo-classical Blender Fiction, filled with television shoes and flesh-filled skies. **120 pages $10**

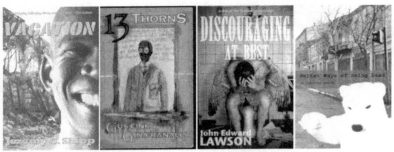

BB-049 **"Vacation" Jeremy C. Shipp** - Blueblood Bernard Johnson leaved his boring life behind to go on The Vacation, a year-long corporate sponsored odyssey. But instead of seeing the world, Bernard is captured by terrorists, becomes a key figure in secret drug wars, and, worse, doesn't once miss his secure American Dream. **160 pages $14**

BB-051 **"13 Thorns" Gina Ranalli** - Thirteen tales of twisted, bizarro horror. **240 pages $13**

BB-050 **"Discouraging at Best" John Edward Lawson** - A collection where the absurdity of the mundane expands exponentially creating a tidal wave that sweeps reason away. For those who enjoy satire, bizarro, or a good old-fashioned slap to the senses. **208 pages $15**

BB-052 **"Better Ways of Being Dead" Christian TeBordo** - In this class, the students have to keep one palm down on the table at all times, and listen to lectures about a panda who speaks Chinese. **216 pages $14**

BB-053 **"Ballad of a Slow Poisoner" Andrew Goldfarb** Millford Mutterwurst sat down on a Tuesday to take his afternoon tea, and made the unpleasant discovery that his elbows were becoming flatter. **128 pages $10**

BB-054 **"Wall of Kiss" Gina Ranalli** - A woman... A wall... Sometimes love blooms in the strangest of places. **108 pages $9**

BB-055 **"HELP! A Bear is Eating Me" Mykle Hansen** - The bizarro, heartwarming, magical tale of poor planning, hubris and severe blood loss... **150 pages $11**

BB-056 **"Piecemeal June" Jordan Krall** - A man falls in love with a living sex doll, but with love comes danger when her creator comes after her with crab-squid assassins. **90 pages $9**

BB-057 **"Laredo" Tony Rauch** - Dreamlike, surreal stories by Tony Rauch. **180 pages $12**

BB-058 **"The Overwhelming Urge" Andersen Prunty** - A collection of bizarro tales by Andersen Prunty. **150 pages $11**

BB-059 **"Adolf in Wonderland" Carlton Mellick III** - A dreamlike adventure that takes a young descendant of Adolf Hitler's design and sends him down the rabbit hole into a world of imperfection and disorder. **180 pages $11**

BB-060 **"Super Cell Anemia" Duncan B. Barlow** - "Unrelentingly bizarre and mysterious, unsettling in all the right ways..." - Brian Evenson. **180 pages $12**

BB-061 **"Ultra Fuckers" Carlton Mellick III** - Absurdist suburban horror about a couple who enter an upper middle class gated community but can't find their way out. **108 pages $9**

BB-062 **"House of Houses" Kevin L. Donihe** - An odd man wants to marry his house. Unfortunately, all of the houses in the world collapse at the same time in the Great House Holocaust. Now he must travel to House Heaven to find his departed fiancee. **172 pages $11**

BB-063 **"Necro Sex Machine" Andre Duza** - The Dead Bitch returns in this follow-up to the bizarro zombie epic Dead Bitch Army. **400 pages $16**

BB-064 **"Squid Pulp Blues" Jordan Krall** - In these three bizarro-noir novellas, the reader is thrown into a world of murderers, drugs made from squid parts, deformed gun-toting veterans, and a mischievous apocalyptic donkey. **204 pages $12**

BB-065 **"Jack and Mr. Grin" Andersen Prunty** - "When Mr. Grin calls you can hear a smile in his voice. Not a warm and friendly smile, but the kind that seizes your spine in fear. You don't need to pay your phone bill to hear it. That smile is in every line of Prunty's prose." - Tom Bradley. **208 pages $12**

BB-066 **"Cybernetrix" Carlton Mellick III** - What would you do if your normal everyday world was slowly mutating into the video game world from Tron? **212 pages $12**

BB-067 **"Lemur" Tom Bradley** - Spencer Sproul is a would-be serial-killing bus boy who can't manage to murder, injure, or even scare anybody. However, there are other ways to do damage to far more people and do it legally... **120 pages $12**

BB-068 **"Cocoon of Terror" Jason Earls** - Decapitated corpses...a sculpture of terror...Zelian's masterpiece, his Cocoon of Terror, will trigger a supernatural disaster for everyone on Earth. **196 pages $14**

BB-069 **"Mother Puncher" Gina Ranalli** - The world has become tragically over-populated and now the government strongly opposes procreation. Ed is employed by the government as a mother-puncher. He doesn't relish his job, but he knows it has to be done and he knows he's the best one to do it. **120 pages $9**

BB-070 **"My Landlady the Lobotomist" Eckhard Gerdes** - The brains of past tenants line the shelves of my boarding house, soaking in a mysterious elixir. One more slip-up and the landlady might just add my frontal lobe to her collection. **116 pages $12**

BB-071 **"CPR for Dummies" Mickey Z.** - This hilarious freakshow at the world's end is the fragmented, sobering debut novel by acclaimed nonfiction author Mickey Z. **216 pages $14**

BB-072 **"Zerostrata" Andersen Prunty** - Hansel Nothing lives in a tree house, suffers from memory loss, has a very eccentric family, and falls in love with a woman who runs naked through the woods every night. **144 pages $11**

BB-073 **"The Egg Man" Carlton Mellick III** - It is a world where humans reproduce like insects. Children are the property of corporations, and having an enormous ten-foot brain implanted into your skull is a grotesque sexual fetish. Mellick's industrial urban dystopia is one of his darkest and grittiest to date. **184 pages $11**

BB-074 **"Shark Hunting in Paradise Garden" Cameron Pierce** - A group of strange humanoid religious fanatics travel back in time to the Garden of Eden to discover it is invested with hundreds of giant flying maneating sharks. **150 pages $10**

BB-075 **"Apeshit" Carlton Mellick III** - Friday the 13th meets Visitor Q. Six hipster teens go to a cabin in the woods inhabited by a deformed killer. An incredibly fucked-up parody of B-horror movies with a bizarro slant. **192 pages $12**

BB-076 **"Rampaging Fuckers of Everything on the Crazy Shitting Planet of the Vomit At smosphere" Mykle Hansen** - 3 bizarro satires. Monster Cocks, Journey to the Center of Agnes Cuddlebottom, and Crazy Shitting Planet. **228 pages $12**

BB-077 **"The Kissing Bug" Daniel Scott Buck** - In the tradition of Roald Dahl, Tim Burton, and Edward Gorey, comes this bizarro anti-war children's story about a bohemian conenose kissing bug who falls in love with a human woman. **116 pages $10**

BB-078 **"MachoPoni" Lotus Rose** - It's My Little Pony... *Bizarro* style! A long time ago Poniworld was split in two. On one side of the Jagged Line is the Pastel Kingdom, a magical land of music, parties, and positivity. On the other side of the Jagged Line is Dark Kingdom inhabited by an army of undead ponies. **148 pages $11**

BB-079 **"The Faggiest Vampire" Carlton Mellick III** - A Roald Dahl-esque children's story about two faggy vampires who partake in a mustache competition to find out which one is truly the faggiest. **104 pages $10**

BB-080 **"Sky Tongues" Gina Ranalli** - The autobiography of Sky Tongues, the biracial hermaphrodite actress with tongues for fingers. Follow her strange life story as she rises from freak to fame. **204 pages $12**

BB-081 **"Washer Mouth" Kevin L. Donihe** - A washing machine becomes human and pursues his dream of meeting his favorite soap opera star. **244 pages $11**

BB-082 **"Shatnerquake" Jeff Burk** - All of the characters ever played by William Shatner are suddenly sucked into our world. Their mission: hunt down and destroy the real William Shatner. **100 pages $10**

BB-083 **"The Cannibals of Candyland" Carlton Mellick III** - There exists a race of cannibals that are made of candy. They live in an underground world made out of candy. One man has dedicated his life to killing them all. **170 pages $11**

BB-084 **"Slub Glub in the Weird World of the Weeping Willows" Andrew Goldfarb** - The charming tale of a blue glob named Slub Glub who helps the weeping willows whose tears are flooding the earth. There are also hyenas, ghosts, and a voodoo priest **100 pages $10**

BB-085 **"Super Fetus" Adam Pepper** - Try to abort this fetus and he'll kick your ass! **104 pages $10**

BB-086 **"Fistful of Feet" Jordan Krall** - A bizarro tribute to spaghetti westerns, featuring Cthulhu-worshipping Indians, a woman with four feet, a crazed gunman who is obsessed with sucking on candy, Syphilis-ridden mutants, sexually transmitted tattoos, and a house devoted to the freakiest fetishes. **228 pages $12**

BB-087 **"Ass Goblins of Auschwitz" Cameron Pierce** - It's Monty Python meets Nazi exploitation in a surreal nightmare as can only be imagined by Bizarro author Cameron Pierce. **104 pages $10**

BB-088 **"Silent Weapons for Quiet Wars" Cody Goodfellow** - "This is high-end psychological surrealist horror meets bottom-feeding low-life crime in a techno-thrilling science fiction world full of Lovecraft and magic..." -John Skipp **212 pages $12**

BB-089 **"Warrior Wolf Women of the Wasteland" Carlton Mellick III**
Road Warrior Werewolves versus McDonaldland Mutants...post-apocalyptic fiction has never been quite like this. **316 pages $13**

BB-090 **"Cursed" Jeremy C Shipp** - The story of a group of characters who believe they are cursed and attempt to figure out who cursed them and why. A tale of stylish absurdism and suspenseful horror. **218 pages $15**

BB-091 **"Super Giant Monster Time" Jeff Burk** - A tribute to choose your own adventures and Godzilla movies. Will you escape the giant monsters that are rampaging the fuck out of your city and shit? Or will you join the mob of alien-controlled punk rockers causing chaos in the streets? What happens next depends on you. **188 pages $12**

BB-092 **"Perfect Union" Cody Goodfellow** - "Cronenberg's THE FLY on a grand scale: human/insect gene-spliced body horror, where the human hive politics are as shocking as the gore." -John Skipp. **272 pages $13**

BB-093 **"Sunset with a Beard" Carlton Mellick III** - 14 stories of surreal science fiction. **200 pages $12**

BB-094 **"My Fake War" Andersen Prunty** - The absurd tale of an unlikely soldier forced to fight a war that, quite possibly, does not exist. It's Rambo meets Waiting for Godot in this subversive satire of American values and the scope of the human imagination. **128 pages $11**

BB-095**"Lost in Cat Brain Land" Cameron Pierce** - Sad stories from a surreal world. A fascist mustache, the ghost of Franz Kafka, a desert inside a dead cat. Primordial entities mourn the death of their child. The desperate serve tea to mysterious creatures. A hopeless romantic falls in love with a pterodactyl. And much more. **152 pages $11**

BB-096 **"The Kobold Wizard's Dildo of Enlightenment +2" Carlton Mellick III** - A Dungeons and Dragons parody about a group of people who learn they are only made up characters in an AD&D campaign and must find a way to resist their nerdy teenaged players and retarded dungeon master in order to survive. 232 **pages $12**

BB-097 **"My Heart Said No, but the Camera Crew Said Yes!" Bradley Sands** - A collection of short stories that are crammed with the delightfully odd and the scurrilously silly. **140 pages $13**

BB-098 **"A Hundred Horrible Sorrows of Ogner Stump" Andrew Goldfarb** - Goldfarb's acclaimed comic series. A magical and weird journey into the horrors of everyday life. **164 pages $11**

BB-099 **"Pickled Apocalypse of Pancake Island" Cameron Pierce** A demented fairy tale about a pickle, a pancake, and the apocalypse. **102 pages $8**

BB-100 **"Slag Attack" Andersen Prunty** - Slag Attack features four visceral, noir stories about the living, crawling apocalypse. A slag is what survivors are calling the slug-like maggots raining from the sky, burrowing inside people, and hollowing out their flesh and their sanity. **148 pages $11**

BB-101 **"Slaughterhouse High" Robert Devereaux** - A place where schools are built with secret passageways, rebellious teens get zippers installed in their mouths and genitals, and once a year, on that special night, one couple is slaughtered and the bits of their bodies are kept as souvenirs. **304 pages $13**

BB-102 **"The Emerald Burrito of Oz" John Skipp & Marc Levinthal** OZ IS REAL! Magic is real! The gate is really in Kansas! And America is finally allowing Earth tourists to visit this weird-ass, mysterious land. But when Gene of Los Angeles heads off for summer vacation in the Emerald City, little does he know that a war is brewing...a war that could destroy both worlds. **280 pages $13**

BB-103 **"The Vegan Revolution... with Zombies" David Agranoff** When there's no more meat in hell, the vegans will walk the earth. **160 pages $11**

BB-104 **"The Flappy Parts" Kevin L Donihe** - Poems about bunnies, LSD, and police abuse. You know, things that matter. 132 **pages $11**

ORDER FORM

TITLES	QTY	PRICE	TOTAL

Please make checks and moneyorders payable to ROSE O'KEEFE / BIZARRO BOOKS in U.S. funds only. Please don't send bad checks! Allow 2-6 weeks for delivery. International orders may take longer. If you'd like to pay online via PAYPAL.COM, send payments to publisher@eraserheadpress.com.

SHIPPING: US ORDERS - $2 for the first book, $1 for each additional book. For priority shipping, add an additional $4. INT'L ORDERS - $5 for the first book, $3 for each additional book. Add an additional $5 per book for global priority shipping.

Send payment to:

BIZARRO BOOKS
C/O Rose O'Keefe
205 NE Bryant
Portland, OR 97211

Address

City   State   Zip

Email   Phone